The Man With the Black Feather

The Man With the Black Feather

Gaston Leroux

MINT EDITIONS

The Man With the Black Feather was first published in 1903.

This edition published by Mint Editions 2021.

ISBN 9781513271965 | E-ISBN 9781513276960

Published by Mint Editions®

minteditionbooks.com

Publishing Director: Jennifer Newens
Design & Production: Rachel Lopez Metzger
Project Manager: Micaela Clark
Translated by Edgar Jepson
Typesetting: Westchester Publishing Services

Contents

I

M. Theophrastus Longuet Desires to Improve His Mind and Visits Historical Monuments

M. Theophrastus Longuet was not alone when he rang the bell of that old-time palace prison, the Conciergerie: he was accompanied by his wife Marceline, a very pretty woman, uncommonly fair for a Frenchwoman, of an admirable figure, and by M. Adolphe Lecamus, his best friend.

The door, pierced by a small barred peephole, turned heavily on its hinges, as a prison door should; the warder, who acts as guide to the prison, dangling a bunch of great old-fashioned keys in his hand, surveyed the party with official gloom, and asked Theophrastus for his permit. Theophrastus had procured it that very morning at the Prefecture of Police; he held it out with the air of a citizen assured of his rights, and regarded his friend Adolphe with a look of triumph.

He admired his friend almost as much as he admired his wife. Not that Adolphe was exactly a handsome man; but he wore an air of force and vigour; and there was nothing in the world which Theophrastus, the timidest man in Paris, rated more highly than force and vigour. That broad and bulging brow (whereas his own was narrow and high), those level and thick eyebrows, for the most part raised a trifle to express contempt of others and self-confidence, that piercing glance (whereas his own pale-blue eyes blinked behind the spectacles of the short-sighted), that big nose, haughtily arched, those lips surmounted by a brown, curving moustache, that strong, square chin; in a word, all that virile antithesis to his own grotesque, flabby-cheeked face, was the perpetual object of his silent admiration. Besides, Adolphe had been Post-Office Inspector in Tunis: he had "crossed the sea."

Theophrastus had only crossed the river Seine. No one can pretend that that is a real crossing.

The guide set the party in motion; then he said:

"You are French?"

Theophrastus stopped short in the middle of the court.

"Do we look like Germans?" he said with a confident smile, for he was quite sure that he was French.

"It's the first time I ever remember French people coming to visit the Conciergerie. As a rule French people don't visit anything," said the guide with his air of official gloom; and he went on.

"It is wrong of them. The monuments of the Past are the Book of History," said Theophrastus sententiously; and he stopped short to look proudly at his wife and Adolphe, for he found the saying fine.

They were not listening to him; and as he followed the guide, he went on in a confidential tone, "I am an old Parisian myself; and if I have waited till to-day to visit the monuments of the Past, it was because my business—I was a manufacturer of rubber stamps right up to last week—did not give me the leisure to do it till the hour I retired from it. That hour has struck; and I am going to improve my mind." And with an air of decision he struck the time-old pavement with the ferule of his green umbrella.

They went through a little door and a large wicket, down some steps, and found themselves in the Guard-room.

They were silent, abandoning themselves entirely to their reflections. They were doing all they could to induce these old walls, which recalled so prodigious a history, to leave a lasting impression on their minds. They were not insensible brutes. While the guide conducted them over Cæsar's tower, or Silver tower, or Bon Bec tower, they told themselves vaguely that for more than a thousand years there had been in them illustrious prisoners whose very names they had forgotten. Marceline thought of Marie Antoinette, the Princess Elizabeth, and the little Dauphin, and also of the waxwork guards who watch over the Royal Family in museums. In spirit therefore she was in the Temple while she was in body visiting the Conciergerie. But she did not suspect this; so she was quite happy.

As they descended the Silver tower, where the only relict of the Middle Ages they had found was an old gentleman on a stool in front of a roll-top desk, classifying the documents relating to political prisoners under the Third Republic, they came once more into the Guard-room on their way to Bon Bec tower.

Theophrastus, who took a pride in showing himself well-informed, said to the guide: "Wasn't it here that the Girondins had their last meal? You might show us exactly where the table was and where Camille Desmoulins sat. I always look upon Camille Desmoulins as a personal friend of mine."

"So do I," said Marceline with a somewhat superior air.

Adolphe jeered at them. He asserted that Camille Desmoulins was not a Girondin. Theophrastus was annoyed, and so was Marceline. When Adolphe went on to assert that Camille Desmoulins was a Cordelier, a friend of Danton, and one of the instigators of the September massacres, she denied it.

"He was nothing of the kind," she said firmly. "If he had been, Lucie would never have married him."

Adolphe did not press the point, but when they came into the Torture-chamber in Bon Bec tower, he pretended to be immensely interested by the labels on the drawers round the walls, on which were printed "Hops," "Cinnamon," "Senna."

"This was the Torture-chamber; they have turned it into a dispensary," said the guide in gruff explanation.

"They have done right. It is more humane," said Theophrastus sententiously.

"No doubt; but it's very much less impressive," said Adolphe coldly.

At once Marceline agreed with him. . .

One was not impressed at all. . . They had been expecting something very different. . . This was not at all what they had looked for.

But when they came on to the Clock platform, their feelings underwent a change. The formidable aspect of those feudal towers, the last relics of the old Frankish monarchy, troubles for awhile the spirit of even the most ignorant. This thousand-year-old prison has witnessed so many magnificent death-agonies and hidden such distant and such legendary despairs that it seems that one only has to penetrate its depths to find sitting in some obscure corner, damp and fatal, the tragic history of Paris, as immortal as those walls. That is why, with a little plaster, flooring, and paint, they have made there the office of the Director of the Conciergerie and that of the Recorder; they have put the ink-spiller in the place once occupied by the executioner. It is, as Theophrastus says, more humane.

None the less, since, as Adolphe affirmed, it is less impressive, that visit of the 16th of last June threatened to leave on the minds of the three friends nothing but the passing memory of a complete disillusion when there happened an incident so unheard of and so curiously fantastic that I considered it absolutely necessary, after reading Theophrastus Longuet's account of it in his memoirs, to go to the Conciergerie and cross-examine the guide himself.

I found him a stolid fellow, officially gloomy, but with his memory of the events of Theophrastus' visit perfectly clear.

At my questions he lost his air of gloom, and said with some animation, "Everything was going quite as usual, sir; and I had just shown the two gentlemen and the lady the kitchens of St. Louis—where we keep the whitewash. We were on our way to the cell of Marie Antoinette, which is now a little chapel. The figure of Christ before which she must have prayed is now in the Director's office—"

"Yes, yes; let's get to the facts!" I interrupted.

"We're just coming to them. I was telling the gentleman with the green umbrella that we had been compelled to put the Queen's armchair in the Director's office because the English were carrying away all the stuffing of it in their purses—"

"Oh, cut out the English!" I said with some impatience.

He looked at me with an injured air and went on: "But I must tell you what I was saying to the gentleman with the green umbrella when he interrupted me in such a strange tone that the other gentleman and the lady cried out together, 'What's the matter, Theophrastus? I never heard you speak like that before! *I shouldn't have recognised your voice!*'"

"Ah! and what was he saying to you?"

"We had come just to the end of Paris Street—you know the passage we call Paris Street at the Conciergerie?"

"Yes, yes: get on!"

"We were at the top of that dreadful black passage where the grating is behind which they used to cut off the women's hair before guillotining them. It's the original grating, you know."

"Yes, yes: get on!"

"It's a passage into which a ray of sunlight never penetrates. You know that Marie Antoinette went to her death down that passage?"

"Yes, yes: cut out Marie Antoinette!"

"There you have the old Conciergerie in all its horror. . . Then the gentleman with the green umbrella said to me, '*Zounds! It's Straw Alley!*'"

"He said that? Are you sure? Did he really say '*Zounds*'?"

"Yes, sir."

"Well, after all, there's nothing very remarkable in his saying, '*Zounds! It's Straw Alley!*'"

"But wait a bit, sir," said the guide with yet more animation. "I answered that he was wrong, that Straw Alley was what we to-day call 'Paris Street.' He replied in that strange voice: '*Zounds! Are you going to teach me about Straw Alley? Why, I've slept on the straw there, like the others!'* I said laughing, though I felt a bit uncomfortable, that no one had slept in Straw Alley for more than two hundred years."

"And what did he say to that?"

"He was going to answer when his wife interfered and said: 'What are you talking about, Theophrastus? Are you going to teach the guide his business when you've never been to the Conciergerie before in your life?' Then he said, but in his natural voice, the voice in which he had been speaking since they came in: 'That's true. I've never been to the Conciergerie in my life.'"

"What did he do then?"

"Nothing. I could not explain the incident, and I thought it all over, when something stranger still happened. We had visited the Queen's cell, and Robespierre's cell, and the chapel of the Girondins, and that little door through which the prisoners of September went to get massacred in the court; and we had come back into Paris Street. On the left-hand side of it there's a little staircase which no one ever goes down, because it leads to the cellars; and the only thing to see in the cellars is the eternal night which reigns there. The door at the bottom of this is made of iron bars, a grating—perhaps a thousand years old, or even more. The gentleman they called Adolphe was walking with the lady towards the door of the Guard-room, when without a word the gentleman with the green umbrella ran down the little staircase and called up from the bottom of it in that strange voice I was telling you about:

"'Hi! Where are you going to? *It's this way!*'

"The other gentleman, the lady, and myself stopped dead as if we had been turned to stone. I must tell you, sir, that his voice was perfectly awful; and there was nothing in his appearance to make one expect such a voice. I ran, in spite of myself as it were, to the top of the staircase. The man with the green umbrella gave me a withering glance. Truly I was thunderstruck, turned to stone and thunderstruck; and when he shouted to me, 'Open this grating!' I don't know how I found the strength to rush down the stairs and open it. Then, when the grating was opened, he plunged into the night of the cellars. Where did he go? How did he find his way? That basement of the Conciergerie is plunged in a terrible darkness which nothing has broken for ages and ages."

"Didn't you try to stop him?" I said sharply.

"He had gone too far; and I hadn't the strength to stop him. *The man with the green umbrella just gave me orders*; and I had to obey him. And we stood there for a quarter of an hour, half out of our wits: it was so odd. And his wife talked, and his friend talked, and I talked; and we said nothing of any use; and we stared into the darkness till our eyes ached. Suddenly we heard his voice—not his first voice, but his second voice, the awful voice—and I was so overcome, I had to hang on to the bars of the door.

"'Is that you, *Simon the Auvergnat*?' he cried.

"I didn't answer anything; and as he went past me, I fancied he put a scrap of paper into his breast pocket. He sprang up the staircase three steps at a time; and we went up after him. He did not offer any explanation; and I simply ran to open the door of the prison for them. I wanted to see their backs. When the wicket was opened and the man with the green umbrella was crossing the threshold, he said, for no reason that I could see:

"'*We must avoid the wheel.*'

"There was no carriage passing."

II

The Scrap of Paper

What did happen? The matter is very obscure. I cannot do better than give Theophrastus Longuet's account of it in the actual words of his memoirs in the sandalwood box.

"I am a man with a healthy mind in a healthy body," he writes, "and a good citizen: that is, I have never transgressed the law. Laws are necessary; and I have always kept them. At least I believe I have.

"I have always hated the imagination; and by that I mean that in all circumstances, whether, for instance, it has been a case of conferring my friendship on anyone, or of having to decide on a line of conduct, I have always been careful to stick to common sense. The most simple always seemed to me the best.

"I suffered deeply, for instance, when I discovered that my old College friend Adolphe Lecamus was addicted to the study of Spiritualism.

"The man who says Spiritualism says rubbish. To try to question spirits by turning tables is utterly absurd. I know what I am talking about, for, wishing to prove the absurdities of his theories, I have taken part in séances with Adolphe and my wife. We sat for hours round a little table which absolutely refused to turn. I laughed at him heartily; and that annoyed my wife, because women are always ready to put faith in the impossible and believe in the mysterious.

"He used to bring her books which she read greedily; and sometimes he would amuse himself by trying to send her to sleep by making passes before her face. I have never seen anything sillier. I should not indeed have stood it from anyone else; but I have a strong liking for Adolphe. He has a powerful face; and he has been a great traveller.

"He and Marceline called me a sceptic. I answered that I was not a sceptic in the sense of a man who believes in nothing or doubts everything. I believe in everything worthy of belief; for example, I believe in Progress. I am not a sceptic; I am a philosopher.

"During his travels Adolphe read a great deal; I manufactured rubber stamps. I am what people call 'an earthy spirit.' I do not make a boast of it; I merely state it.

"I thought it well to give this sketch of my character to make it clear that what happened yesterday is no fault of mine. I went to see the prison as I might have gone to buy a neck-tie at the Louvre. I wished to improve my mind. I have plenty of spare time nowadays, since we have sold the business. I said, 'Let us do as the English do and see the sights of Paris.' It was a mere chance that we began with the Conciergerie.

"I am very sorry indeed that we did.

"Am I really very sorry? I am not sure. I am not sure of anything. At present I am quite calm. And I am going to write down what happened exactly as if it had happened to someone else. All the same, what a story it is!

"While we were going through the towers nothing happened worth setting down here. I remember saying to myself in Bon Bec tower:

"'What, was it here in this little chamber, which looks just like a grocery, that there were so many agonies and so many illustrious victims martyred?'

"I tried honestly to picture to myself the horror of that chamber when the executioner and his assistants with their horrible instruments came to the prisoners with the intention of forcing them to confess crimes affecting the state. But owing to the little labels on the drawers, on which one reads 'Senna,' 'Hops,' I did not succeed.

"That Bon Bec tower! They used also to call it *The Prattler* on account of the horrible cries which burst from it and made the quiet passer-by shudder and quicken his steps along the quay at the sound of the King's justice.

"Now Bon Bec tower is peaceful and very still. I am not complaining of it: it is Progress.

"But when we penetrated to that part of the Conciergerie which has hardly changed for centuries and were walking quietly along between those bare stone walls which no fresh facing, no profane plaster has ever covered, an inexplicable fever began to fill my veins; and when we were in the gloom at the end of Straw Alley, I cried, '*Zounds! It's Straw Alley!*'

"At once I turned to see who had spoken those words. They were all staring at me; and I perceived plainly that I had spoken them myself. Indeed, my throat was still quivering from their utterance.

"The idiot of a guide asserted that we had passed Straw Alley. I contradicted him; and he shut up. I was sure of my facts, you understand, quite sure that it was Straw Alley. I told him that I had slept on the straw in it. But it is absurd. How do you suppose I could have slept on straw in Straw Alley when it was the first time I had ever been in the Conciergerie? Besides, was I sure? That is what worries me. I had an atrocious headache.

"My brow was burning even while I felt it swept by a strong current of cold air. Outside I was cool; inside I was a furnace.

"What had we been doing? I had a moment before walked quietly through the chapel of the Girondins; and while the guide was telling us the history of it, I played with my green umbrella. I was not in the least annoyed at having just behaved so oddly. I was my natural self. But as for that, I have never ceased to be my natural self.

"That which befell me later was also quite natural, since it was not the result of any effort. The unnatural is exactly what did not befall me.

"I remember finding myself at the bottom of a staircase in front of a grating. I was endowed with superhuman vigour; I shook the grating and shouted, 'This way!' The others, *who did not know*, were slow coming. I do not know what I should have done to the grating, if the guide had not unlocked it for me. For that matter, I do not know what I should have done to the guide. I was mad. No: I have no right to say that. I was not mad; and that's a great pity. It is worse than if I had been mad.

"Undoubtedly I was in a state of great nervous excitement; but my mind was quite lucid. I do not believe that I have ever seen so clearly; and yet I was in the dark. I do not believe that I have ever had clearer recollections; and yet I was in a place I did not know. Heavens! I did not recognise it and *I did recognise it*! I did not hesitate about my way. My groping hands found the stones they reached out in the darkness to find; and my feet trod a soil which could not have been strange to them.

"Who will ever be able to tell the age of that soil; who will ever be able to tell you the age of those stones? *I do not know it myself.* They talk of the origin of the palace. What is the origin of the old Frankish palace? They may be able to say when those stones will end; they will never be able to say when they began. And they are forgotten, those stones, in the thousand-year night of the cellars. The odd thing is that I remembered them.

"I crept along the damp walls as if the way were well known to me. I expected certain rough places in the wall; and they came to the tips of my fingers; I counted the edges of the stones and I knew that at the end of a certain number I had only to turn to see at the far end of a passage *a ray which the sun had forgotten there since the beginning of the history of*

Paris. I turned and saw the ray; *and I felt my heart beat loudly from the bottom of the centuries*."

M. Longuet interrupts his narrative for a while to describe the whirl of his mind during this singular hour. He has the greatest difficulty in remaining master of his thought, the utmost difficulty in following it. It rushes on in front of him like a bolting horse whose reins he has let go. It leaves him behind and bounds ahead, leaving on the paper, as traces of its passage, words of such profundity that when he looks at them, he says, they make him giddy.

And he adds, in a paroxysm of dread:

"One must stop on the edge of these words as one stops on the edge of a precipice."

And he guides the pen with a feverish hand, as he goes on burying himself in the depths of these subterranean galleries:

"And that's the Prattler! These are the walls which have heard! It was not up above, in the sunlight, that the Prattler spoke; it was here, in this night of the underworld. Here are the rings in the walls. Is it the ring of Ravaillac? *I no longer remember*.

"But towards the ray, towards the unique ray, motionless and eternal, the faint, square ray, which from the beginning of ages took and preserved the form of the air-hole, I advance; I advance in a stumbling hurry, while the fever consumes me, blazes, and dizzies my brain. My feet stop, but with such a shock that one would believe them caught by invisible hands, risen from the soil; my fingers run over the wall, groping and fumbling that spot in the wall. What do my fingers want? What is the thought of my fingers? I had a pen-knife in my pocket; and all at once I let my green umbrella fall to the ground to take my pen-knife from my pocket. And I scraped, with certainty, between two stones. I cleared away the dust and mortar from between two stones. Then my knife pierced a thing between the two stones and brought it out.

"That is why I know I am not mad. That thing is under my eyes. In my quietest hours, I, Theophrastus Longuet, can look at it on my desk between my latest models of rubber stamps. It is not I who am mad; it is this thing that is mad. It is a scrap of paper, torn and stained—a document whose age there is no telling and which is in every way calculated to plunge a quiet manufacturer of rubber stamps into the wildest consternation. The paper, as you can guess, is rotted by the damp of the cellars. The damp has eaten away half the words, which seem from their red hue to have been written in blood.

"But in these words before me, in this document which was certainly written two centuries ago, which I passed under the square ray from the air-hole and gazed at with my hair rising on end in horror, I Recognised My Own Handwriting."

Here copied clearly out is this precious and mysterious document:

"I rt uried
my treasures after betrayal
of April 1st
Go and take the air
at the Chopinettes
look at the Gall
look at the Cock
Dig on the spot and you
will be rich."

III

Theophrastus Longuet Bursts into Song

On leaving the prison, Marceline and Adolphe were, very naturally, full of curiosity to learn the reasons of Theophrastus' extraordinary behaviour; and he had the greatest difficulty in getting them away from the subject. He treated the matter lightly, declaring that the whim had taken him to visit the cellars of the Conciergerie; and he had visited them. They were even more impressed by his attitude to the guide than by his actual plunge into the cellars. That Theophrastus, the timid Theophrastus, should have browbeaten not a mere man, but an official, amazed them. Theophrastus admits that he was as much amazed as they, and felt rather proud of himself. All the evening they kept recurring to the matter until their amazement and their interest began to weaken by mere continuance of expression. But Theophrastus was glad indeed when sleep at last tied Marceline's tongue.

The next day he shut himself up in his study on the pretext of straightening out his accounts. Its window looks down on to the little grass-plot in the middle of Anvers Square; and he leaned out over the sill, contemplating the prosaic reality of the scene as if he could not have enough of it. He was above all pleased by the nurses wheeling along their babies in perambulators and by the shouting of the children romping about the Square.

His thought was of a great unity and a great simplicity. It was entirely contained in the phrase: "The World has not changed."

No: the world had not changed. There were the babies in the perambulators; and as the clock struck two the Signora Petito, wife of the Professor of Italian who occupied the flat above his, began to play *The Carnival of Venice*.

No: nothing in the world had changed; yet when he turned round, he could see on his desk, among the models of rubber stamps, a scrap of paper.

Did that scrap of paper *really* exist? He had passed a feverish night, almost a night of delirium; and at the end of it he had decided that his strange adventure must have been a bad dream. But in the morning he had found the scrap of paper in a drawer of his desk. . .

Even now he kept saying to himself, "I shall turn round presently; and the scrap of paper won't be there." He turned round; and the scrap of paper was there—*in his own handwriting*.

He passed his hand over his perspiring brow and heaved the sigh of a grieved child. Then he seemed to come to a definite resolve and carefully put the scrap of paper into his pocket-book. He had just remembered that Signor Petito had a great reputation as an expert in handwriting. His friend Adolphe was also an expert in handwriting, but from the Spiritualistic point of view. He told the character by it. Theophrastus had no intention of calling Adolphe into counsel. There was already too much mystery in the affair to entrust it to the overflowing imagination of a medium who boasted himself a pupil of a Papus.

He went slowly upstairs and was ushered into Signor Petito's study.

He found himself in the presence of a man of middle age, whose chief characteristics were a mass of crinkly black hair, a piercing glance, and enormous ears. After they had exchanged greetings, Theophrastus broached the subject of the scrap of paper. He drew it from his pocket-book and an unsigned letter which he had written a few days previously.

"Signor Petito," he said, "I understand that you are a first-class expert in handwriting. I should be much obliged if you would examine this letter and this document, and inform me of the result of your examination. I assert myself that there is no connection—"

He stopped short, as red as a peony, for he was not in the habit of lying. But Signor Petito had already scanned the letter and the scrap of paper with the eye of an expert; and with a smile which showed all his exceedingly white teeth, he said:

"I won't keep you waiting for my answer, M. Longuet. The document is in a very bad state; but the scraps of handwriting one can read are in every respect the same as the handwriting of the letter. Before the Courts, M. Longuet, before God and before men, these two handwritings were traced *by the same hand*!" He laid his hand on his heart with a great air.

He entered into particulars: a child, he declared, could not make a mistake about it. He became oracular.

"The handwriting in both is equally angular," he said in a very pompous tone. "By angular, M. Longuet, we describe a handwriting in which the thin strokes which join the strokes of the letters and the letters to one another are at an acute angle. You understand? Look at this hook, and this one, and this thin stroke, and all these letters which increase progressively in equal proportions. But what an acute handwriting, M. Longuet! I have never seen handwriting so acute: *it's as sharp as the blade of a knife*!"

At these last words Theophrastus turned so pale that Signor Petito thought that he was going to faint. None the less he took the letter and the document, thanked Signor Petito, and went out of the flat.

He walked straight out of the house and wandered about the streets for a long while. At last he found himself in Saint-Andrew-des-Arts Place; then he took his way to Suger Street, and opened the latch of an old-fashioned door. He found himself in a dark and dirty passage. A man came down it to meet him, and recognising him, greeted him.

"How are you, Theophrastus? What good wind blows you here?" he said in affectionate tones.

"How are you, Ambrose?" said Theophrastus gloomily.

Since they had not met for two years, they had a hundred inquiries to make of one another. Ambrose was an engraver of visiting-cards by profession. He had been a printer in the Provinces; but having put all his capital into a new invention in printing, it had not been long before he found himself a bankrupt. He was a cousin of Marceline; and Theophrastus, who was a good soul, had come to his aid in the hour of his gravest trouble.

Theophrastus sat down on a straw-seated chair in a little room which served as workshop, and was lighted by a large, dusty skylight in the ceiling.

"You 're a scientific man, Ambrose," he said, still gloomily.

"Nothing of the kind!" said Ambrose quickly.

"Yes; you are. No one could teach you anything in the matter of paper."

"Oh, yes: that's true enough. I do know paper."

"You know all papers," said Theophrastus.

"All," said Ambrose with modest pride.

"If one showed you a piece of paper you could tell the age of it?"

"Yes; I have published a monograph on the water-marks of the papers used in France during the seventeenth and eighteenth centuries. The Academy crowned it."

"I know it. And I have the fullest confidence in your knowledge of papers," said Theophrastus with unrelieved gloom.

"It's well-founded; but really it's a very simple matter. The oldest papers presented at first, when they were new, a smooth, glossy surface. But soon wire-marks appeared in them, crossed at regular intervals by perpendicular lines, both reproducing the impression of the metal trellis on which the paste was spread. In the fourteenth century they had the idea of utilising this reproduction by making it a mark of the source or mill which the paper came from. With this object in view, they embroidered in brass wire on the trellis mould, initials, words, and all kinds of emblems: these are the water-marks. Every water-marked sheet of paper carries in itself its birth-certificate; but the difficulty is to decipher it. It requires a little practice: the pot, the eagle, the bell. . ."

Theophrastus opened his pocket-book and held out his scrap of paper with trembling fingers.

"Could you tell me the exact age of this document?" he said.

Ambrose put on his spectacles and held the paper up to the light.

"There's a date," he said. "172. . . The last figure is missing. It would be a paper of the eighteenth century then. Given the date within ten years, our task becomes very simple."

"Oh, I saw the date," said Theophrastus quickly. "But is this really an eighteenth-century paper? Isn't the date false? That's what I want to know."

Ambrose pointed to the middle of the scrap.

"Look," he said.

Theophrastus looked; but he saw nothing. Then Ambrose lighted a little lamp and threw its light on the document. In holding the scrap of paper between one's eyes and the lamp one distinguished in the middle of it a kind of crown.

"This paper's extremely rare, Theophrastus!" cried Ambrose in considerable excitement. "This water-mark is almost unknown, for very little of it was manufactured. The water-mark is called 'The Crown of Thorns.' This paper, my dear Theophrastus, is exactly of the year 1721."

"You are sure of it?"

"Absolutely. But how comes it that this document, which is dated 1721, is, in every part of it which is visible, in your handwriting?" cried Ambrose in a tone of amazement.

Theophrastus rose, put the document back into his pocket-book, and went out on stumbling feet, without answering.

I reproduce from the medley of documents of which his memoirs are composed the following passage:

"So now," writes Theophrastus, "I had the proof; I could no longer doubt; I had no longer the right to doubt. This scrap of paper which dated from the beginning of the eighteenth century, from the times of the Regent, this sheet which I had found, or rather *had gone to seek* in a prison, was truly in my own handwriting. I had written on this sheet, I, Theophrastus Longuet, late manufacturer of rubber stamps, who had only retired the week before, at the age of forty-one years, I had written on this sheet the still incomprehensible words which I read on it, in 1721! Besides, I had not really any need of Signor Petito, or of Ambrose, to assure me of it. All my being cried, 'It's your paper! It's your paper!'"

"So before being Theophrastus Longuet, the son of Jean Longuet, market-gardener at Ferté-sous-Jouarre, I had been in the past someone whom I did not know, but who was re-born in me. Yes: every now and then I 'foamed at the mouth' at remembering that I lived two hundred years ago!

"Who was I? What was then my name? I had a strange certainty that these questions would not remain unanswered for long. Was it not a fact that already things of which in my present existence I was ignorant, were rising from my past? What did certain phrases I had uttered at the Conciergerie mean? Who was Simon the Auvergnat, whose name had risen twice to my burning lips?

"Yes, yes: the name of long ago, *my* name, would also rise to my awakening brain; and knowing who I was, I should recall the whole of my reviving life in the past, and read the document at a glance."

Theophrastus Longuet might well be troubled in mind. He was a simple, rather dense, self-satisfied soul who had never believed in anything but rubber stamps. A good-natured, strictly honest, narrow-minded and obstinate tradesman, like the bulk of his class in France he had considered religion only fit for women; and without declaring himself an unbeliever, he had been wont to say that when one died one was dead for a long time.

He had just learned in the most convincing, palpable fashion that *one was never dead*.

It was indeed a blow. But he took it very well. From the moment that he remembered having been alive at the beginning of the eighteenth century, he began to regret that it was not two thousand years earlier.

That is the nature of the French tradesman; he is full of common sense; but when he does exaggerate, he passes all bounds.

In his uncertainty about his previous existence he had two definite facts to start from: the date 1721, and the Conciergerie prison. These enabled him to affirm that in 1721 he had been confined in the Conciergerie as a Prisoner of State: he could not admit for an instant that even in the wicked times of Louis XV he, Theophrastus Longuet, could possibly have been in prison for an offence against the Common Law.

Again the scrap of paper gave grounds for certain inferences. At some desperate conjuncture, possibly on the eve of his execution, he had written it and hidden it in the wall, to find it on a passing visit, two centuries later. There was nothing supernatural about that; it was merely the logical explanation of the facts of the case.

He betook himself once more to the consideration of the document. Two words in it seemed to him, naturally, of paramount importance. They were the words "Betrayal" and "Treasures."

He hoped from these two words to reconstitute his earlier personality. In the first place, it was plain that he had been rich and powerful. Only rich men bury treasures; only powerful men are betrayed. It seemed to him that it must have been a memorable, perhaps historic betrayal, of *the betrayal of the First of April.*

Whatever else was mysterious about the document, it was quite clear that he had been a great personage and had buried treasures.

"By Jove!" he said to himself. "Provided that no one has touched them, those treasures belong to me! If need were, with this document in my own handwriting I could establish my claim to them."

Theophrastus was not a rich man. He had retired from business with a moderate competence: a cottage in the country, with its little garden, its fountain, and its lawn. It was not much, with Marceline's occasional fits of extravagance. Decidedly the treasures would come in very useful.

At the same time we must give him the credit of being far more interested in the mystery of his personality than in the mystery of the treasures. He decided to postpone his search for them till he could definitely give a name to the personage who had been Theophrastus in 1721. To his mind this discovery, which was of chief interest to him, would be the key to all the rest.

He was somewhat astonished by the sudden disappearance of what he called his "historical instinct." It had been lacking during the earlier part of his life; but it had revealed itself to him in the cellars of the Conciergerie with the suddenness and emphasis of a clap of thunder. For a while the Other (in his mind he called the great personage he had been in the eighteenth century the "Other") had taken possession of him. The Other had been so completely master of him that he had acted with the Other's hands and spoken with his voice. It was the

Other who had found the document. It was the Other who had cried, "*Zounds! It's Straw Alley!*" It was the Other who had called *Simon the Auvergnat* and then had vanished. Theophrastus did not know what had become of him. He sought in vain. He sounded himself, plumbing the depths of his being. Nothing!

Theophrastus would not stand it. He had not been troubled all his life long by any unhealthy curiosity about the beginning or end of things; he had wasted no time on the mysteries of philosophy. He had shrugged his shoulders at their futility. But since the revelation of the extraordinary fact that a man sold rubber stamps in 1911 after burying treasures in 1721, he swore to go to the end of the business. He would know. He would know everything.

His "historical instinct" seemed to have left him for the time being, he would hunt for it in books. He would assuredly end by finding out who was the mysterious personage who had been shut up in the Conciergerie in 1721 after having been betrayed on the First of April. Which First of April? That remained to discover.

Little as the selling of rubber stamps fits man for historical research, he betook himself to libraries and hunted for that personage. He studied the lives of the chief men of the period. Since he was at it, nothing was too grand for him: Princes, Peers, Statesmen, and Generals, he studied the lives of all. He paused for a while at the great financier Law, but found him too dissipated; the same objection applied to the Comte du Barry; and he was positively horrified by the thought that he might have been the Comte de Charolais, renowned for his debaucheries, whose hobby was to shoot thatchers at work on the house-roofs. For forty-eight hours he was the Cardinal de Polignac before he was disgusted to learn that that great Churchman had not been a man of stainless virtue. Whenever he did find a person whom the historians painted in the most engaging colours and adorned with the most solid virtues, that personage invariably disobliged him by not having been shut up in the Conciergerie or betrayed on the First of April.

However he had just discovered, *in the Journal de Barbier*, a favourite of the Regent who, strangely enough, was exactly the man he was looking for, when there came a development of his case which plunged him into a profound consternation.

He had sent Marceline down to his country cottage on the banks of the Marne, to which it was their habit to betake themselves at the beginning of July; and Adolphe had gone down to the village inn, to help her get it in order for their stay. Their absence left him freer to prosecute his researches. Then on the morning of the anniversary of his wedding-day he went down to join them at the cottage. He had called it "Azure Waves Villa," in spite of the remonstrances of Adolphe, who had urged that such a name was only suitable to a cottage by the sea. Theophrastus had been firm in the matter because, he declared, he had often been to Treport, and the sea was always green; whereas, fishing for gudgeon in the Marne, he had frequently observed that its waves were blue.

He found his wife and friend awaiting him eagerly on its threshold; and as with the air of a favourite of the Regent, he complimented Marceline on her charming appearance, he gracefully waved his green umbrella, from which he seldom allowed himself to be parted, in the fashion in which he believed the dandies waved their canes at the beginning of the eighteenth century.

He found the household in the stress of the preparations for the anniversary dinner, to which several of his friends in the neighbourhood brought their wives to do honour to Theophrastus and Marceline.

Still the favourite of the Regent, to the astonishment of Marceline and Adolphe, he found a few gracious words of compliment for each guest. Neither of them had ever seen him so shine as host before.

They dined in a tent in the garden; and the talk at once turned on fishing, a sport to which they were all devoted; and they did their best to be accurate about their exploits. M. Lopard had caught a three-pound pike; old Mlle. Taburet complained bitterly that someone had been fishing in her favourite pool; a third declared that the fish were being overfed; and there was a long discussion on ground-bait.

Theophrastus said nothing: he suddenly found these good people too middle-class for him. He would have liked to raise the level of the conversation; and he would have preferred it to deal with the matters which filled his fevered imagination.

Towards the end of dinner he found a way to set Adolphe talking of ghosts. Then Madame Lopard told them of the extraordinary doings of a somnambulist who lived near; and at once Adolphe explained the phenomena of somnambulism according to the Spiritualistic theory, and quoted Allan Kardec. Adolphe was never at a loss to explain "phenomena." Then, at last, they came to the matter to which Theophrastus was burning to bring them, the Transmigration of Souls.

Marceline observed that our reason rejected the hypothesis; and Adolphe protested vigorously: "Nothing is lost in nature," he said authoritatively. "Everything is transformed, souls and bodies alike. The transmigration of souls with a view to their purification is a belief which goes back to the remotest antiquity; and the philosophers of all ages have been careful not to deny it."

"But if one came back into a body, one would know it," said Marceline.

"Not always, only sometimes," said Adolphe confidently.

"Sometimes? Is that so?" said Theophrastus quickly; and his heart began to beat tumultuously.

"Oh, yes: there are instances—authentic instances," said Adolphe emphatically. "Ptolemy Cæsarion, Cleopatra's son and King of Egypt thirty years before Christ, recollected perfectly that he had been the philosopher Pythagoras who lived six hundred years before him."

"Impossible!" cried the ladies; and the men smiled with an air of superior wisdom.

"It's nothing to laugh at, gentlemen. It's the most serious subject in the world," said Adolphe sternly. "The actual transformation of our bodies which is the last word in Science, is in entire accord with the theory of Reincarnation. What is this theory of transformation except that living beings *transform themselves into one another*? Nature for ever presents herself to us as a creative flame unceasingly perfecting types, on her way to the attainment of an ideal which will be the final crown of the Law of Progress. Since Nature has only one aim, what she does for bodies, she does also for souls. I can assure you that this is the case, for I have studied this question, which is the very foundation of all sound Science."

None of the party understood Adolphe's discourse, a fact which filled him with quiet pride; but they listened to him in an ecstasy; and he was pleased to see that Theophrastus, as a rule so restive under such discussions, was listening with the liveliest interest. It was an attitude hardly to be wondered at in a man who was hearing that what seemed a wild imagining of his delirium rested on a firm scientific basis.

"The transmigration of souls was taught in India, the cradle of the human race," Adolphe continued in his most professorial tone, delighted to have caught the ear of the party. "Then it was taught in Egypt, then in Greece by Pythagoras. Plato took the doctrine from him; and adduced irrefutable proofs in his Phædo that souls do not pass into eternal exile but return to animate new bodies."

"Oh, if we could only have proofs of a fact like that!" cried Madame Sampic, the wife of the schoolmaster of Pont-aux-Dames, with enthusiasm.

"If we had, I shouldn't mind dying one bit," said old Mlle. Taburet, who was in mortal fear of her approaching end.

"There *are* proofs—irrefutable proofs," said Adolphe solemnly. "There are two: one drawn from the general order of Nature, one from human consciousness. Firstly, Nature is governed by the law of contradictions, says Plato, meaning by that that when we see in her bosom death succeed life we are compelled to believe that life succeeds death. Is that clear to you?"

"Yes, yes," cried several of the guests, without understanding a word he was saying.

"Moreover, Plato continues, since nothing can be born from nothing, if the beings we see die were never to return to life, everything would end by becoming absorbed in death, and Nature would be moving towards an eternal sleep. Have I made this first proof clear?"

"Yes, yes: the second!" cried his fellow guests, quite untruthfully.

"Secondly," said Adolphe, growing absolutely pontifical, "when, after having observed the general laws of the Universe, we descend into the depths of our own being, we find the same dogma confirmed by the fact of memory. 'To learn,' cries Plato to the Universe, 'To learn is nothing else but to remember.' Since our soul learns, it is that it remembers. And what does it remember if not that it has lived before, and that it has lived in another body? 'Why should we not believe that in quitting the body which it animates at the moment, it must animate several others in succession?' I am quoting Plato word for word," said Adolphe in a tone of ringing triumph.

"And Plato is a person to be reckoned with," said Theophrastus warmly.

"Charles Fourier says," said Adolphe, moving on to the modern, "Where is the old man who does not desire not to be certain of carrying into another life the experience he has acquired in this one? To assert that this desire can never be realised is to admit that the Deity would deceive us. We must then recognise that we have lived already, before being what we are to-day, and that many more lives await us. All these lives—Fourier adds with a precision for which we cannot be sufficiently thankful—to the number of a hundred and ten are distributed over five stages of unequal extent and cover a period of eighty-one thousand years."

"Eighty-one thousand years! That's pretty filling!" interrupted M. Lopard.

"We spend twenty-seven thousand of them on our planet and the other fifty-four thousand elsewhere," explained Adolphe.

"And how long is it before we come back into another body?" asked Madame Bache.

"At least two or three thousand years, if we are to believe Allan Kardec, always supposing that we have not died a violent death. Then, especially if one has been executed, one may be reincarnated at the end of two hundred years," said Adolphe.

"That's it! They must have hanged me," said Theophrastus to himself. "Or if they didn't hang a man of my quality, they beheaded me. All the same," he went on to think, with a natural pride, "if these people here knew that they were sitting with a favourite of the Regent, or perhaps a Prince of Royal blood, how astonished and respectful they'd be! But not a bit of it: they are merely saying to themselves, 'It's Theophrastus Longuet, manufacturer of rubber stamps'; and that's enough for them."

The advent of the two waiters with the champagne cut short the dissertation of Adolphe; and though everyone had been deeply impressed by it, now they only wished to be amused.

It was then that Marceline turned to Theophrastus and begged him to sing the song with which he was wont to delight their ears at dessert on each anniversary of their wedding-day. He had sung it on their wedding-day itself; and thanks to its charm and freshness, it had been a great success. It was Beranger's *Lisette*.

But what was the amazement of Marceline and all the guests, when Theophrastus sprang to his feet, threw his napkin on the table, and bawled to the mistress of the house:

"As you will, *Marie-Antoinette*! I can refuse you nothing!"

"Gracious goodness! *That voice of his has come back!*" gasped Marceline.

The guests had not recovered from the shock when Theophrastus bawled to an old French air, in a voice which none of them recognised as his, his voice of the Conciergerie, bawled to the most select society from Crécy-en-Brie to Lagny-Thorigny-Pomponne:

"Bullies all! In our snug cribs
We live like fighting-cocks:
On dainties rich we splash the dibbs,
And booze we never docks.

Then guzzle, cullies, and booze away
Till Gabriel's trump on Judgment Day!"

In spite of the richness of the rhyme, no applause followed the stanza. The ladies did not clink their glasses with their knives; they stared at Theophrastus with their eyes starting out of their heads; and the eyes of Marceline projected furthest of all.

Theophrastus did not need any applause; like one possessed of a devil, he bawled on:

"Bullies all! In our snug cribs
Dan Cupid loves to dance.
He brings to help us splash the dibbs
The prettiest silk in France.
Then guzzle, cullies, and booze away
Till Gabriel's trump on Judgment Day!"

In a final triumphant roar he repeated the last couplet and prolonged the final note, his eyes on the sun, which was sinking over the edge of the horizon, laid one hand on his heart, embraced "Nature" with a sweeping gesture of the other, and bellowed:

"Then guzzle, cullies, and booze away
Till Gabriel's trump on Judgment Day!"

He sat down with an air of supreme content, and said proudly:

"*What do you think of that, Marie-Antoinette?*"

"Why do you call me Marie-Antoinette?" gasped the trembling Marceline.

"Because you're the prettiest of them all!" roared Theophrastus in that awful voice. "I appeal to Madame la Maréchale de Boufflers, who's a woman of taste! I appeal to all of you! And there's not one of you, by the Pope's gullet, who'll dare to deny it! Neither the big Picard, nor the Bourbonnais, nor the Burgundian, nor Sheep's-head, nor the Cracksman, nor Parisian, nor the Provincial, nor the little Breton, nor the Feather, nor Patapon, nor Pint-pot, nor St. James's Gate, nor Gastelard, nor Iron-arm, nor Black-mug, nor even Fancy Man!"

Since Theophrastus had on his right old Mlle. Taburet, he prodded her in the ribs by way of emphasis, an action which nearly made her faint.

No one dared budge; his flaming eye chained them to their chairs; and leaning affectionately towards Mlle. Taburet, he pointed to the gasping Marceline, and said:

"Look, Mlle. Taburet, aren't I right? Who can compare with her? Pretty-Milkmaid, of Pussycat? Or even Blanche, the Bustler? Or Belle-Hélène who keeps the Harp tavern?"

He turned towards Adolphe.

"Here—you—old Easy-Going!" he said with a terrifying energy. "Let's have your opinion. Look at Marie-Antoinette a moment! By the Sucking-pig! there's not one to compare with her: not Jenny Venus, the flower-seller of the Palais-Royal, nor Marie Leroy, nor mother Salomon, the pretty coffee-house-keeper of the Temple, nor Jenny Bonnefoy *who's just married Veunier who keeps the Pont-Marie café*. Not one of them, I tell you! Not one of them! The Slapper, Manon de Versailles, Fat-Poulteress, the Lock, Cow-with-the-Baskets, or the Bastille!"

With a bound Theophrastus was on the table; and the crockery round him smashed into a thousand pieces. He caught up a glass and bellowed:

"I drink to the queen of the nymphs! Marie-Antoinette Neron!"

He crushed the glass in his hands, cutting them in twenty places, and bowed to the company.

But the company had fled.

IV

Adolphe Lecamus is Flabbergasted But Frank

Theophrastus stood on the table and gazed sheepishly round the empty tent. His fine ardour was extinguished.

But I take up the narrative in the words of his memoirs:

"I found myself on the table," he writes, "in the middle of the broken crockery, and all the company fled. My guests' rough fashion of taking leave of me had confused me a little. I wished to get down, but by a singular phenomenon, I found as much difficulty in getting down from the table as I had displayed address in mounting it. I went down on my hands and knees; and by dint of the most careful precautions reached the ground safely. I called Marceline, who did not answer; and presently I found her trembling in our bedroom. I shut the door carefully and set about explaining matters. Her appealing eyes, full of tears, demanded an explanation; and I felt it my duty as a husband to hide from her no longer my great and amazing trouble of mind.

"'My dear Marceline,' I said, 'you must be entirely at a loss to understand what happened this evening; but never mind, I don't understand it myself. Still, by putting our heads together, reinforced by our love for one another, I do not despair of arriving at the correct explanation of it.'

"Then I coaxed her to go to bed; and when at last her head rested peacefully on the pillow, I told her my story. I gave her a complete account of my visit to the cellars of the Conciergerie, concealing nothing, and describing exactly the extraordinary feelings which troubled me and the unknown force which appeared to control me. At first she said nothing; in fact she seemed to shrink away from me as if she were frightened of me; but when I came to the document in the wall which revealed the existence of the treasures, at once she asked to see it.

"I took it from my pocket-book, and showed it to her by the light of the moon, which was at its full. Like myself, like all who had already seen it, she recognised my handwriting; and crossed herself for all the world as if she suspected something diabolical in it.

"However the sight of the document seemed to relieve her; and at once she said that it was most fortunate that we had at hand an expert in Spiritualism, that Adolphe would be of the greatest service to us in this difficult matter. We had the paper on the bed before us in the moonlight; and in the presence of this unshakable witness, she was presently compelled to admit that I was a reincarnated soul dating from two hundred years before.

"Then, as I was once more asking who I could have been, she annoyed me for the first time since our marriage.

"'Poor Theophrastus, you couldn't have been up to much,' she said.

"'And why not?' I said sharply, for I was nettled.

"'Because, dear, this evening you sang a song in slang; and the ladies whose names you mentioned certainly couldn't have belonged to the Aristocracy. When one associates with the Slapper, the Lock, and Manon of Versailles, one can't be up to much.'

"She said this in a tone of contempt which I put down to jealousy.

"'But I also spoke of La Maréchale de Boufflers,' I said again rather sharply. 'And you ought to know that in the time of the Regent all the ladies of the Court had some queer nickname. It's my belief, on the contrary, that I was a man of quality—what do you say to a favourite of the Regent?'

"I spoke rather huffily; and she gave me a kiss, and admitted that there was a good deal in what I said.

"The next morning she repeated her suggestion that we should take Adolphe into our confidence. She declared that his wide experience in these matters and his profound knowledge of metaphysics could not but be of the greatest help to a man who had buried treasures two hundred years ago and wished to recover them.

"'You'll see, dear, that he's the man who'll tell you what your name was,' she said.

"I yielded to her persuasion; and as we sat in the garden after lunch, I explained to him the inner meaning of the strange occurrence of the evening before. I took him back from the song to the document, from the document to the Conciergerie, watching the effect of the astonishing revelation on the expression of his face. It was clear that he was utterly astounded; and it appeared to me very odd that a professed Spiritualist should be so flabbergasted at finding himself face to face with a retired man of business, sound in mind and body, who claimed to have existed two hundred years before. He said that my behaviour at yesterday's dinner and the incomprehensible phrases to which I had given utterance at the Conciergerie were indeed calculated to prepare him for such a confidence, but as a matter of fact he had not been expecting anything of the kind, and was entirely nonplussed. He would like to have actually in his hand the proofs of such a phenomenon.

"I took out my document and handed it to him. He could not deny its authenticity; he recognised the handwriting. Indeed that recognition drew a sharp explanation from him; and I asked him the reason of it. He answered that my handwriting on a document two hundred years old explained a heap of things.

"'What things?' I said.

"He confessed loyally that till that moment he had never understood my handwriting and that it had always been impossible for him to see any connection between it and my character.

"'Is that so?' I said. 'And what is your conception of my character, Adolphe?'

"'Well, you won't be angry, if I'm frank with you?' he said, hesitating.

"'Of course not,' I said.

"On this assurance he described my character: it was that of a worthy business man, an honest merchant, an excellent husband, but of a man incapable of displaying any firmness, strength of mind, or energy. He went on to say that my timidity was excessive, and that my kindness of heart, to which he was fully alive, was always apt to degenerate into sheer feebleness.

"It was not a flattering portrait; and it made me blush for myself.

"'And now,' said I, hiding my mortification, 'you've told me what you think of my character: what do you think of my handwriting?'

"'It's the exact opposite of your character,' he said quickly. 'It expresses every sentiment utterly opposed to your nature as I know it. In fact, I can't think of a more direct antithesis than your character and your handwriting. It must be, then, that you haven't the handwriting which goes with your actual character, but the handwriting of the Other.'

"I might have been angry, if Signor Petito had not told me much the same thing; as it was, I exclaimed, 'Oh, this is very interesting! The Other, then, was a man of energy?'

"I thought to myself that the Other must have been some great leader. Then Adolphe went on; and as long as I live I shall never forget his words, so painful did I find them:

"'Everything shows, these thin strokes, the way they are joined to one another, their manner of rising, mounting, topping one another, energy, strength of will, pigheadedness, harshness, ardour, activity, ambition. . . for evil.'

"I was dismayed; but in a flash of genius I cried:

"'What is evil? What is good? If Attila had known how to write, he might have had the handwriting of Napoleon!'

"'Attila was called "the flail of God,"' he said.

"'And Napoleon was the flail of men,' I retorted on the instant.

"I was hard put to it to restrain my anger; but I asserted that *Theophrastus Longuet could only be an honest man before this life, during this life, and after this life*.

"My dear wife agreed with me, warmly. Adolphe saw that he had gone too far, and apologised."

V

Theophrastus Shows the Black Feather

From that day the conversations of Theophrastus, Marceline, and Adolphe were of fascinating interest to them. They pored and pored over the document; they discussed over and over again the "Cock," the "Gall," "Chopinettes," and the "Betrayal of April 1st" of the mysterious document. They soon left Azure Waves Villa and returned to Paris to ransack the libraries.

Adolphe, the great reader, was much better adapted to historical research than either Marceline or Theophrastus; and their patience was exhausted long before his.

One Sunday they were strolling along the Champs-Elysées; and both Theophrastus and Marceline had been complaining bitterly of their failure at the libraries, when Adolphe said thoughtfully:

"What use would it be to us to find approximately the spot in which the treasures are buried *unless Theophrastus had his Black Feather*?"

"What Black Feather? What do you mean?" said Marceline and Theophrastus with one voice.

"Let's stroll back towards the Rond-Pont; and I'll tell you what I mean," said Adolphe.

When they were under the trees, among the throng of careless strollers, Adolphe said:

"You've heard of the water-finders?"

"Of course," they said promptly.

"Well, owing to some phenomenon, of which the explanation has not yet been discovered, these water-finders, equipped with forked hazel-twigs which they hold over the ground they are crossing, are able to *see*, through the different strata of the soil, the position of the spring sought, and the spot where the well must be sunk. I don't despair of getting Theophrastus to do for his treasures what the water-finders do for their springs. I shall take him to the place, and he will say, 'Here's where you dig for the treasures.'"

"But all this does not explain what you mean by my Black Feather," interrupted Theophrastus.

"I'm coming to it. I shall bring to this spot you, the treasure-seeker, as one brings the water-finder to the spot where one suspects the presence of water. I shall bring you there *when you have your Black Feather*."

He paused, and then went on in his professorial tone:

"I shall have to talk to you about Darwin; but you needn't be uneasy: I shan't have to talk about him for long. You'll understand at once. You know that Darwin devoted a great part of his life to some famous experiments of which the most famous were his experiments with pigeons. Desirous of accounting for the phenomena of heredity, he studied closely the breeding of pigeons. He chose pigeons because the generations of pigeons follow one another so closely that one can draw conclusions from them in a comparatively short space of time. At the end of a certain number, call it X, of generations he found once more the same pigeon. You understand, the same pigeon, with the same defects and the same qualities, the same shape, the same structure, and *the same black feather* in the very place where the first pigeon had a black feather. Well, I, Adolphe Lecamus, maintain, and I will prove it to you, that to eyes opened by Darwin it is the same with souls as with bodies. At the end of a number X of generations, one finds the same soul, exactly as it was originally, with the same defects and the same qualities, *with the same black feather*. Do you understand?"

"Not quite," said Theophrastus apologetically.

"Yet I'm lowering myself to the level of your intelligence," said Adolphe, impatient but frank. "But it is necessary to distinguish between the soul which appears hereditarily and that which returns by reincarnation."

"What do you mean?" said Theophrastus rather faintly.

"An hereditary soul which revives the ancestor *has always its black feather*, owing to the fact that it is the result of a unique combination, since it exists in the sheath, the body, which is hereditary to the same extent. Is that clear?"

"I notice that whenever you say, 'Is that clear?' my dear Adolphe, everything seems to go as dark as pitch," said Marceline humbly.

Adolphe ground his teeth, and raised his voice:

"Whereas a soul which returns in the course of reincarnation finds itself in a body in which nothing has been prepared to receive it. The aggregate of the materials of this body have their origin in—I take Theophrastus as example—several generations of cabbage-planters—"

"Gardeners—market-gardeners!" interjected Theophrastus gently.

"—at Ferté-sous-Jouarre. The aggregate of the materials of this body may for a while impose silence on this soul, originally perhaps—I am still taking Theophrastus as an example—belonging to one of the first families in France. But there comes a time when the soul gets the upper hand; then it speaks, and shows itself in its entirety, exactly as it was originally, *with its black feather*."

"I understand! I understand the whole business!" cried Theophrastus joyfully.

"Then when this soul speaks in you," cried Adolphe, warming to eloquence, "you're no longer yourself! Theophrastus Longuet has disappeared! It's the Other who is there! The Other who has the gestures, the air, the action, and *the Black Feather* of the Other! It's the Other who will recall exactly the mystery of the treasures! It's the Other who remembers the Other!"

"Oh, this is wonderful!" cried Theophrastus, almost in tears of joy. "I grasp now what you mean by my *Black Feather*. I shall have *my Black Feather* when I'm the Other!"

"And we will help you in the matter, dear friend," said Adolphe with unabated warmth. "But till we have disentangled the Unknown who is hidden in Theophrastus Longuet, until he is alive before our very eyes with the right amount of force, daring, and energy, until, in a word, he appears with *his Black Feather*, let us calmly devote ourselves to the study of this interesting document which you brought back from the Conciergerie. Let us make it our pastime to penetrate its mystery, let us fix the limits of the space in which these treasures were buried. But let us wait before ransacking the bowels of the earth till the Other, who is asleep in you, awakes and cries, 'It is here!'"

"You speak like a book, Adolphe!" cried Marceline, overwhelmed with admiration. "But can we really expect the soil in which the treasures were buried to have remained undisturbed all these years—over two hundred?"

"Woman of little faith," said Adolphe sternly, "they have been disturbing the sacred soil of the Roman Forum for over two thousand years as the soil of Paris has never been disturbed; and it was only a few years ago that they brought to light the famous rostrum from which Caius and Tiberius poured forth their eloquence. . . Ah, here's M. Mifroid, my friend the Commissary of Police, whom I've so long wanted you to know. Well, this is lucky!"

A man of forty, dressed in the height of fashion and as neat as a new pin, with one white lock drawn carefully down on his unwrinkled brow, came up to them smiling, raised his hat, and shook Adolphe warmly by the hand.

"How are you?" said Adolphe cordially. "Let me introduce you to my friends. M. Mifroid—Madame Longuet—M. Longuet."

From the glance of respectful admiration which he bestowed on her charming face Marceline gathered that the Commissary of Police was also a squire of dames.

"We have often heard our friend M. Lecamus speak of you," she said with a gracious smile.

"I feel that I have known you for a long time. Every time I meet him, he talks about his friends of Gerando Street, and in such terms that the good fortune which this moment befalls me, this introduction, has been my most fervent desire," said M. Mifroid gallantly.

"I hear that you are an accomplished violinist," said Marceline, delighted with his politeness.

"Accomplished? I don't know about accomplished: I *play* the violin; and I am something of a sculptor and a student of philosophy—a taste which I owe to our friend M. Lecamus here. And when I passed you just now, I heard you discussing the immortality of the soul," said M. Mifroid, who wished to shine before the eyes of the pretty Marceline.

"Adolphe and I love to discuss these serious questions; and just now we were discussing the body and soul and the relations between them," said Theophrastus with a very fair imitation of the professorial air of Adolphe.

"Haven't you got beyond that?" said M. Mifroid, burning to shine. "In the eyes of Science matter and spirit are one and the same thing, that is to say, they constitute the same unity in the same Force, at once result and phenomenon, cause and effect, moving towards the same end: the Progressive Ascent of Being. You two gentlemen are the only people left to make this distinction between matter and spirit."

Theophrastus was a trifle huffed: "We do the best we can," he said stiffly.

The little party had come into the Place de la Concorde. At the top of the Rue Royale there was a large crowd of people, shouting and gesticulating.

At once Theophrastus, like a true Parisian, was on fire to learn what was going on, and plunged into the heart of the crowd.

"Mind you don't get your pockets picked!" cried Marceline after him.

"Oh, you needn't be afraid of getting your pocket picked when you're in the company of Commissary Mifroid," said that gentleman proudly.

"That's true," said Marceline with an amiable smile. "You are here; and we run no risk at all."

"I don't know about that," said Adolphe slyly. "My friend Mifroid appears to me more dangerous than all the pickpockets on the face of the earth—to the heart."

"Ah, he will have his joke!" said M. Mifroid laughing; but he assumed his most conquering air.

Theophrastus kept them standing there for fully ten minutes before he emerged from the crowd with his eyes shining very brightly.

"It's a cab-driver who has locked his wheel with that of a motor car," he said.

"And what has happened?" said Marceline.

"Why, he can't unlock it," said Theophrastus.

"And all this crowd about a trifle like that! How silly people are!" said Marceline.

Thereupon she invited M. Mifroid to come home and dine with them. He needed but a little pressing to accept the invitation; and they strolled slowly back to Gerando Street.

The dinner was very lively, for M. Mifroid was still bent on shining; and his example spurred Adolphe to splendid emulation. It was when they were taking their coffee at the end of dinner that M. Mifroid suddenly seemed uneasy. He felt in all his pockets, trying to find his handkerchief. His search was vain; it was not there. After a final search in the pockets in the tails of his frock-coat, he ground his teeth, gave his moustache a despairing tug, and took a deep breath.

Two minutes later Theophrastus blew his nose. Marceline asked him where he had got that pretty handkerchief. M. Mifroid looked at it and saw that it was his. He laughed somewhat awkwardly, declared that it was an excellent joke, took it from Theophrastus, and put it in his pocket. Theophrastus could not understand it at all.

Suddenly M. Mifroid turned pale, and felt in his left-hand breast pocket.

"Goodness! What has become of my pocket-book?" he cried.

The explanation of its absence was entirely simple: someone had picked the pocket of the Commissary of Police of his pocket-book with five hundred francs in it. M. Mifroid did not so much regret the loss of the five hundred francs as he was furious to find himself ridiculous. Marceline made fun of him gently as she condoled with him on its loss; she could not help it. He was furious indeed.

"Let me lend you any money you want for to-night, M. Mifroid," said Theophrastus amiably.

He pulled out a pocket-book. M. Mifroid uttered a sharp cry: it was his own pocket-book!

Theophrastus turned a rich scarlet. M. Mifroid stared at him, took the pocket-book from his trembling fingers, recovered his five hundred francs, and put them in his pocket.

Then he forthwith began to make a hundred pressing occupations his excuse for taking a hurried leave of them, and said good-bye.

As he was clattering down the staircase, he called back up it, with some heat, to his friend Adolphe, who had hurried out of the flat after him:

"Whoever are these people you have introduced me to?"

Adolphe said nothing; he wiped his perspiring brow.

The clattering footsteps of M. Mifroid died away down the stairs; and he went slowly back into the dining-room. Theophrastus had just finished turning out his pockets. On the table lay three watches, six handkerchiefs, four pocket-books, containing considerable sums of money, and eighteen purses!

VI

The Portrait

The three friends stared at the three watches, the six handkerchiefs, the four pocket-books, and the eighteen purses in a blank and silent consternation.

There was indeed nothing to be said.

A dreadful despair rested on the face of Theophrastus; but he was the first to break the heavy silence.

"My pockets are *quite* empty," he said.

"Oh, Theophrastus—Theophrastus!" moaned Marceline reproachfully.

"My poor friend," said Adolphe; and he groaned.

Theophrastus wiped away the cold sweat from his brow with a handkerchief of which he did not know the owner.

"I see what it is," he said in a despairing tone. "I've had my *Black Feather*."

Marceline and Adolphe said nothing; they were utterly overwhelmed.

Theophrastus looked from one to the other and wiped the glasses of his spectacles. His face cleared a little; and then he said with a faint smile:

"*Perhaps after all, in those days, it was a parlour game.*"

He stuck the index finger of his right hand into his mouth, with him a sign of grave preoccupation of spirit.

Marceline heaved a deep sigh and said, "Take your finger out of your mouth, dear, and tell us how it came about that you had on you three watches, six handkerchiefs, four pocket-books, and eighteen purses, without counting the handkerchief and pocket-book of Commissary Mifroid. I turned your pockets out this morning to brush the linings; and as usual there was nothing in them but a few scraps of tobacco."

"There was a large gathering in the Place de la Concorde. I plunged into it; and I came out of it with all these things. It's quite simple," said Theophrastus.

"And what are we going to do with them?" said Adolphe in solemn tones.

"What do you want me to do with them?" said Theophrastus sharply, for he was recovering a little from the shock. "You don't suppose I'm going to keep them! Is it my habit to keep things which don't belong to me? I'm an honest man; and I have never wronged a soul. You'll take these things to your friend the Commissary of Police. It will be easy enough for him to find the owners."

"And what am I to tell him?" said Adolphe with a harried air.

"Anything you like!" cried Theophrastus, beginning to lose his temper. "Does an honest cabman who finds a pocket-book and fifty thousand francs in his cab and takes them to the Police Station, bother about what he is going to tell the inspector? He says, 'I've found this in my cab,' and that's enough. He even gets a reward. All you have to say is: 'My friend Longuet asked me to bring you these things which he found in his pocket, and he doesn't ask for any reward.'"

He spoke in a tone of impatient contempt for the intelligence of Adolphe, a tone to which Adolphe was quite unused. Adolphe frowned with ruffled dignity and was about to retort sharply, when Marceline kicked him gently under the table, a little kick which said plainly: "Theophrastus is going off his head! Come, friend, to his rescue!"

Adolphe understood the message of that little shoe: the frown faded from his face, leaving on it only an expression of supernal gloom; he looked at the eighteen purses, scratched his nose, and coughed. Then he gazed at Theophrastus and said in very solemn tones:

"What has just happened, Theophrastus, is not natural. We must try to find the explanation of it; we must force ourselves to find the explanation. It's no use shutting our eyes; we must open them, as wide as we can, to the misfortune, if it is misfortune, in order to battle with it."

"What misfortune?" said Theophrastus, suddenly becoming his timid self again, and catching distressfully at Marceline's hand.

"It's always a misfortune to have other people's property in one's pocket," said Adolphe gloomily.

"And what else is there in the pockets of conjurors?" cried Theophrastus with fresh violence. "And conjurors are very honest men; and Theophrastus Longuet is a very honest man! *By the throttle of Madame Phalaris*, he is!"

He shouted this out; then fell back exhausted in his chair.

There was a gloomy silence. Presently he sat up again, and with tears in his eyes said plaintively:

"I feel that Adolphe is right. I am threatened by some great misfortune and I don't know what it is—I don't know what it is!"

He burst into tears; and Marceline and Adolphe strove in vain to comfort him. But after a while he dried his tears, grasped a hand of either, and said in a firmer voice:

"Swear—swear never to abandon me *whatever happens*."

They promised in all good faith; and the assurance seemed to cheer him a little. Then Adolphe asked him to let him see the document again; and he fetched it. Adolphe spread it out before him and studied it intently. Presently he nodded his head sagely and said:

"Do you ever dream, Theophrastus?"

"Do I ever dream? Well, I suppose I do sometimes. But my digestion is so good that I hardly ever remember my dreams."

"Never?" persisted Adolphe.

"Oh, I couldn't go so far as to say never," said Theophrastus. "In fact, I remember having dreamt four or five times in my life. I remember it because I always woke up at the same point in the dream; and it was always the same dream. But how on earth does it affect this business which is worrying us?"

"Dreams have never been explained by Science," said Adolphe solemnly. "It fancies that it has said everything when it has ascribed them to the effect of the imagination. But it gives us no explanation of the quite clear and distinct visions we sometimes have which have nothing whatever to do with the events or preoccupations of the previous day. In particular how are we to account for those visions of actually existing things which one has never seen in the waking state, things of which one has never even thought? Who will dare to say that they are not retrospective visions of events which have taken place before our present existence?"

"As a matter of fact, Adolphe, I can assure you that the things of which I dream—and I remember now that I have dreamt of them three times—are perhaps real in the past or future, but that I have never seen them in the present."

"You understand my point," said Adolphe in a gratified tone. "But what are these things you have dreamt of but never seen?"

"That won't take long to tell and thank goodness for it, for they're not particularly pleasant. I dreamt that I was married to a wife whom I called Marie-Antoinette and who annoyed me extremely."

"And then?" said Adolphe, whose eyes never quitted the document.

"And then I cut her up into little bits," said Theophrastus, blushing faintly.

"What a horrible thing to do!" cried Marceline.

"As a matter of fact it was rather horrible," said Theophrastus. "And then I put the pieces into a basket and was going to throw them into the Seine near the little bridge of the Hôtel-de-Ville. At that point I awoke; and I was jolly glad to awake, for it wasn't a pleasant dream."

"It's awful!" cried Adolphe; and he banged his fist down on the table.

"Isn't it?" said Marceline.

"Not the dream! But I've just succeeded in reading the whole of the first line of the document! That's what's awful!" groaned Adolphe.

"What is it? What have you found out?" cried Theophrastus in a panic-stricken tone as he sprang up to pore over the document.

"It reads *I rt uried my treasures*. And you don't know what that *rt* stands for? Well, I'm not going to tell you till I have made absolutely sure. I shall be absolutely sure by to-morrow. To-morrow, Theophrastus, at two o'clock, meet me at the corner of Guénégaud and Mazarine Streets." He rose. "In the meantime I'll take these things along to my friend Mifroid, who will restore them to their owners. Good-night, and courage, Theophrastus—above everything—courage!"

He shook Theophrastus' hand, with the lingering pressure with which one shakes the hand of a relation of the corpse at a funeral, and departed.

That night Theophrastus did not sleep. While Marceline breathed peacefully by his side, he lay awake staring into the darkness. His own breathing was irregular and broken by deep sighs. A heavy oppression weighed on his heart.

The day dawned on Paris gloomily faint and dirty, throwing over its buildings a sinister veil. In vain did the summer sun strive to penetrate that thick and smoky air. Noon, the hour of its triumph, showed only a dull ball, rolling ingloriously in a sulphurous mist.

At six o'clock Theophrastus suddenly jumped out of bed, and awoke Marceline by a burst of insensate laughter. She asked the reason of his strange mirth; and he answered that Nature had not given him a mouth large enough to laugh at the face Commissary Mifroid, who did not believe in pickpockets, would pull at the sight of Adolphe emptying his pockets of the collection with which he had stuffed them.

Then he went on to say in the tone of an official instructor:

"It's the work of a child to take a purse out of a pocket. If you can't get your hand in, insert a straw covered with bird-lime. That device is excellent in crowd-work."

Marceline sat up in bed and stared at him. Theophrastus had never worn a more natural air. He was pulling on his pants.

"There's a button off the waist-band," he grumbled.

"You terrify me, Theophrastus!" said Marceline in a shaky voice.

"And a good job too!" said her husband, going down on his hands and knees to recover his braces which had fallen under the bed. "One only does good work with a good woman. And I can't do anything with you. You will never be a good bustler."

"A good—what?"

"A good bustler. Next time you go to the Maison-Dorée, buy me a pair of braces. These are rotten. You don't even know what a bustler is. You ought to be ashamed of yourself at your age. A bustler is a person of your sex who is clever at hiding anything one gets hold of in her frock. I never had a better bustler than Jenny Venus."

"My poor child!" groaned Marceline.

An access of furious anger seized Theophrastus. He dashed at the bed brandishing the button-hook, and cried:

"You know—you know perfectly well that I've forbidden anyone to call me '*Child*' ever since the death of Jenny Venus!"

Marceline promised that she would never do it again. But oh, how profoundly she regretted having become, along with her husband, the owner of a document which promised them treasures, but which brought into their home trouble, fear, violence, madness, and the inexplicable. After Marie-Antoinette came Jenny Venus. She was unacquainted with either lady; and she had no desire to make their acquaintance. But Theophrastus spoke of them with a disquieting familiarity. In truth the unexpected phrases which fell from his lips, while filling her with a dread of the Theophrastus of two hundred years ago, made her regret indeed the Theophrastus, so easy to understand, of a few days before. She thought of the theory of Reincarnation with the unkindest feelings.

Theophrastus had finished dressing. He complained bitterly that a tear in his flowered waistcoat had not been mended. Then he said that he would not lunch at home, since he had an appointment to meet his *friend Old Easy-Going*, at the corner of Guénégaud and Mazarine Streets, *to play a trick on a Monsieur de Traneuse, an engineer officer for whom he had a strong dislike*; but since the appointment was after lunch, he thought he would go and *take the air at the Chopinettes mill* first.

Marceline was trembling pitiably. She hardly had the strength to say: "It's very bad weather to go to Chopinettes mill."

"Bah! *I'll leave my green umbrella at home and take my Black Feather with me*," said Theophrastus.

With that he went out, putting the finishing touch to his cravat as he went.

On the staircase he met Signor Petito; and they went down it together. Signor Petito greeted M. Longuet with the most respectful politeness, complained of the state of the weather, and paid him a thousand compliments on his air of good health. Theophrastus responded grumpily to these polite advances; and since, when they came out of the house, Signor Petito showed no intention of quitting him, he asked unpleasantly whether the Signora Petito could not be persuaded to learn some other infernal tune besides the *Carnival of Venice*. Signor Petito affected not to notice his carping tone and replied with an amiable smile that she was just going to begin to practise *The Star of Love*, and she would be charmed in the future to devote her talent to any piece which took M. Longuet's fancy. Then even more amiably he said:

"And which way are you going, M. Longuet?"

Theophrastus looked at him with suspicious disfavour and answered:

"I was going to take a turn round Chopinettes mill; but the weather is certainly too bad for that: so I am going down to the Porkers."

"To the Porkers?" said Signor Petito quickly; and he was going to ask where the Porkers was, when he thought better of it, and said, "So am I."

"Indeed? Indeed?" said Theophrastus, eyeing him strangely. "So you're going to the Porkers too?"

"There or elsewhere: it's all the same to me," said Signor Petito; and he laughed a most amiable laugh.

They walked along side by side in silence for a while, till Signor Petito mustered up his courage to ask a question:

"And how are you getting on with your treasures, M. Longuet?" he said.

Theophrastus turned on him with a savage air, and cried, "What the deuce has it got to do with you?"

"Don't you remember bringing, a little while ago, for my opinion on the handwriting—"

"I remember quite well! But you—you'd jolly well better forget!" interrupted Theophrastus in a tone of dry menace; and he opened his green umbrella.

Signor Petito, entirely unabashed, took shelter under it, saying amiably, "Oh, I didn't ask the question to annoy you, M. Longuet."

They had reached the corner of Martyrs' Street in the Trudaine Avenue; and they turned down it, Theophrastus glowering.

Then he said, "I've an appointment at the Sucking-Pig tavern next to the Porkers' chapel, and here we are, Signor Petito."

"But that's Notre-Dame-de-Lorette and not Porkers' chapel at all!" cried Signor Petito.

"I don't like to be contradicted to my face!" snarled Theophrastus, looking at him with a very evil eye and baring his teeth.

Signor Petito protested that he had no intention in the world of doing anything of the kind.

"To my face—I'm well aware that mine is a valuable head," said Theophrastus, regarding Signor Petito with an air which grew stranger and stranger. "Do you know how much it is worth, Signor Petito, the *Child's* head? No? . . . Well, since an opportunity offers, I'm going to tell you. And while I'm about it, I'll tell you a little story which may be useful to you. Come into the Sucking-Pig."

"B—B—But this is the Café B—B—Boussets," stammered Signor Petito, who was growing frightened.

"The mist has muddled you. You've missed your way among *all these ploughed fields*," said Theophrastus, sitting down on a bench before one of the tables. Then he laughed on a very sinister note, and went on: "So you wanted to annoy me, M. Petito. So much the worse for you. What will you have to drink? A glass of ratafia? The excellent Madame Taconet who keeps this tavern has set aside a bottle for me which will warm your in'ards."

AND AS A WAITER IN his white apron came up to the table, without a change of tone Theophrastus added, "Two draught lagers; and we don't want them all froth."

Thus, without any transition, without even noticing it, did he join his present-day existence to his existence of two hundred years before. Signor Petito was already full of the liveliest regret at having insisted on accompanying a man who fancied he was in the Sucking-Pig tavern, when the waiter brought the beer and set it on the table.

Theophrastus said, "My head is worth twenty thousand francs; and well you know it!"

He accompanied the "And well you know it!" with a bang of his fist on the table which made the glasses ring and Signor Petito jump.

"Don't be frightened, Signor Petito: your beer isn't spilt," Theophrastus went on in a jeering tone. "You know then, my good sir, that my head is worth twenty thousand francs; but you'd better act as if you didn't, or some unpleasantness will befall you. I promised you a story. Well, here it is:

"*Just about two hundred years ago* I was walking along Vaugirard Street, with my hands in my pockets and without a weapon of any kind on me, not even a sword, when a man accosted me at the corner of the street, greeted me with all the politeness imaginable and declared that my face had taken his fancy—just as you said and did, Signor Petito!—that his name was Bidel, and all his friends called him Good Old Bidel, and he had a secret to confide to me. I encouraged him with a friendly tap on the shoulder." At this point Theophrastus fetched Signor Petito such a thump on the shoulder that it drew a short howl from him; and he pulled out his money under the constraining desire to go out and see if the mist had dispersed. "Put away your money, Signor Petito, I'm paying for the drinks!" said Theophrastus sharply; and he went on in his easy, conversational tone. "Well, Good Old Bidel, encouraged by my friendly tap," Signor Petito slipped along the bench, "told me his secret. He whispered in my ear that the Regent had offered twenty thousand francs to anyone who would arrest the *Child*; that he, Good Old Bidel, knew where the *Child* was hiding; that I looked to him to be a man of courage, and that with my help he ought to go pretty near getting that twenty thousand francs. We would share it." Theophrastus paused to laugh a laugh which froze Signor Petito's blood. "Good Old Bidel was not in luck's way, Signor Petito, for I too knew where the *Child* was hiding, since the *Child* was me!" Signor Petito did not believe a word of it. It was his firm opinion that M. Longuet had ceased to be a child months ago. But he dared not say so. "I answered Good Old Bidel that it was a regular windfall, and that I was thankful indeed that he had chanced on me; and I begged him to take me straight to the place where the *Child* was hiding. He said:

"'To-night the *Child* will sleep at the Capucins, at the inn of The Golden Cross.'

"It was true, Signor Petito. Good Old Bidel's information was O.K.; and I congratulated him on it. We were passing a cutler's shop; and I went in, and under the astonished eyes of Good Old Bidel bought *a little penny knife*." The eyes of Theophrastus blazed; and the eyes of Signor Petito blinked. "When we came out into the street, Good Old Bidel asked me what on earth I was going to do with *a little penny knife*. I replied, 'With a little penny knife'"—M. Longuet moved nearer to Signor Petito; Signor Petito moved further from M. Longuet—"'one can always kill a *coppers' nark*!' And I jammed it into his ribs! He waved his arms round like a windmill and fell down dead!"

He laughed his blood-freezing laugh again; but Signor Petito was not attending to it: he had slipped along the bench and under it. He crawled swiftly under bench after bench, to the astonishment of the staff of the café, gained the door, plunged through it, and bolted down the street.

M. Theophrastus Longuet drained his glass and rose. He went to the desk, where Mlle. Bertha was counting the brass disks, and said to her:

"Madame Taconet,"—Mlle. Bertha asked herself with some surprise why M. Longuet called her Madame Taconet; but the question met with no response,—"if that little Petito comes here again, tell him from me that the next time I come across him, *I'll clip his ears for him*."

So saying, Theophrastus stroked the handle of his green umbrella as one strokes the hilt of a dagger, and went out without paying.

There can be no reasonable doubt that Theophrastus had his *Black Feather*.

The fog was still thick. He forgot all about lunching. He walked through the sulphurous mist as in a dream. He crossed the old Quartier d'Antin and what was formerly called Bishop's Town. When he saw dimly the towers of the Trinité, he muttered, "Ah, the towers of Cock Castle!" He was at St. Lazare station when he fancied that he was in "Little Poland." But little by little, as the mist cleared, his dream vanished with it. He had a more accurate idea of things. When he crossed the Seine at Pont-Royal, he had once more become honest Theophrastus, and when he set foot on the left bank of the river he had but a vague memory of what had happened on the other side.

But he had that memory. In fact, when he examined himself closely, he found that he was beginning to experience three different mental states: first, that which arose from his actual existence as an honest manufacturer of rubber stamps; second, that which arose from the sudden and passing resurrection of the *Other*; third, that which arose from memory. While the resurrection of the *Other* was, while it lasted, a terrible business, the memory was a pleasant and melancholy frame of mind, calculated to induce in a sorrowful heart a feeling of gentle sadness and philosophic pity.

As he turned his steps towards Guénégaud Street, he asked himself idly why Adolphe had fixed the corner of Guénégaud and Mazarine Streets as their meeting-place.

He took a round-about way to that corner, for *he could not bring himself to walk along the strip of Mazarine Street* where it runs along the palace of the Institute, formerly the Four Nations. *He did not know the reason of this reluctance.*

He went round by De la Monnaie house, and so came into Guénégaud Street.

Adolphe was awaiting him, with a very gloomy face, at the corner, and slipped his arm into his.

"Have you ever heard anyone speak of someone called the *Child*, Adolphe?" said Theophrastus, after they had greeted one another.

"I have indeed," said Adolphe in a tone as gloomy as his face. "And I know his name, his family name."

"Ah, what is it?" said Theophrastus anxiously.

For all reply Adolphe pushed him along a little passage leading to an old house in Guénégaud Street, a few doors off De la Monnaie house. They went into the house, up a shaky staircase, and into a room in which the window curtains were drawn. It had been darkened purposely. But on a little table in a corner a flickering candle threw its light on a portrait.

It was the portrait of a man of thirty, of a powerful face, with "flashing" eyes. The brow was high, the nose big, the strong, square chin shaven; the large mouth was surmounted by a bristly moustache. On the bushy hair was a cap of wool or rough leather; and the dress appeared to be that of a convict. A coarse linen shirt was half open across the hairy chest.

"Goodness!" said Theophrastus without raising his voice. "How did *my portrait* get into this house?"

"Your portrait?" cried Adolphe. "Are you sure?"

"*Who could be surer than I?*" said Theophrastus calmly.

"Well—well—" said Adolphe Lecamus in a choking voice, his face contorted by an expression of the most painful emotion. "This portrait, which is your portrait, is the portrait of that great eighteenth-century king of thieves, CARTOUCHE!"

Theophrastus stared at the portrait with eyes that opened and opened as a sickly pallor overspread his anguished face; a little grunt broke from his parted lips, and he dropped to the ground in a dead faint.

Adolphe dropped on his knees beside him, unfastened his collar, and slapped his hands vigorously. Then he blew out the candle, turned the portrait with its face to the wall, and opened the window.

Theophrastus was a long time recovering his senses. When he did, his first words were:

"On no account tell my wife, Adolphe!"

VII

The Young Cartouche

On the morrow of this terrible discovery Theophrastus and Marceline sought once more the calm joys of Azure Waves Villa. Theophrastus had not said a word of the shocking business; and Marceline had not dared question him about it so that she was still ignorant of their dreadful misfortune. A blank consternation reigned perpetually on his gentle face; and every now and then tears filled his kind eyes.

Adolphe, who had remained in Paris to make researches into the life of the famous King Of Thieves, was to join them in a couple of days; and the hours till his coming passed gloomily indeed: Marceline pottered about the house, busy with her household tasks; Theophrastus silently prepared his fishing-tackle, and on the afternoon of the second day fished with very little luck.

But the third day dawned bright and sunny; and Theophrastus, who had passed a good night, showed an easier face of less dismayed expression; about his lips hovered a shadow of a smile. Adolphe Lecamus came to Esbly station by the 11.46 train, and was welcomed with transports of joy. They went straight to déjeuner, and did not rise from the table till two o'clock. Marceline once more breathed peacefully in the presence of their faithful friend; and Theophrastus regaled him with a detailed account of his afternoon's impassioned, but unsuccessful, fishing. M. Lecamus said little; but after his coffee he helped himself to a third glass of a curaçoa which he appreciated far more highly than it deserved.

After lunch Theophrastus loaded himself with rods, lines, and bait; Adolphe took the landing-net; they bade Marceline good-bye; and walked down to the Marne with the quiet gait of men who have lunched well.

"I have got everything ready for your afternoon's sport," said Theophrastus, when they reached its banks. "While you fish I will listen to your news and amuse myself by trolling. It's all I'm fit for. I've a can full of minnows under the willows. I am prepared for the worst."

Adolphe said nothing; and when he was baiting his hook, Theophrastus said, with a touch of impatience in his tone, "Well?"

"Well, my news is good and bad," said Adolphe. "But I must warn you that it's more bad than good: no doubt they have invented a good many stories about you; but the truth is bad enough for anything."

"Your information is correct?" said Theophrastus with a sigh.

"I went to the source, the original documents," said Adolphe. "I'll tell you what I learned; *and you can set me right if I go wrong*."

"Go on," said Theophrastus in a tone of patient resignation. "I must make the best of it."

"In the first place *you were born in the month of October, 1693, and you are named Louis-Dominique Cartouche*—"

"There's no point in calling me Cartouche," interrupted Theophrastus, pulling a minnow out of the bait-can. "There's no reason anyone should know it. You know what these country people are: they'd laugh at the idea. Call me the *Child*: I prefer it."

"You agree that *Cartouche* is your real name and not a nickname?" persisted Adolphe.

"Cut it out! Cut it out! It's a vile name!" said Theophrastus impatiently.

"They relate that you were well educated at Clermont College and were a pupil there at the same time as Voltaire. But that's a mere legend: unless you learnt to read from the gipsies, you never learnt to read at all."

"I like that!" cried Theophrastus. "How could I have learnt to write unless I knew how to read? And if I didn't know how to write, how could I have written the document I hid in the cellars of the Conciergerie?"

"That's reasonable enough. But at your trial—"

"Did I have a trial?" interrupted Theophrastus eagerly.

"I should think you did—a very famous trial!" said Adolphe. "And at your trial you declared that you did not know how to write. You signed all your depositions with a cross, and you never wrote a line to a single soul."

"Because one never should put anything in writing," said Theophrastus firmly. "I was doubtless afraid to compromise myself. None the less the document exists."

"That's true. But let us go back to your eleventh year. One day you went with some of your school-fellows to Saint-Laurent fair—"

"Look here, Adolphe: couldn't you put it differently? You keep saying, '*You* went with your school-fellows to Saint-Laurent fair'. . . '*You* were born in 1693'. . . 'You were a school-fellow of Voltaire.' After all, though I admit I was *Car*—" he stopped short—"the *Child*, I am also Theophrastus Longuet; and I can assure you that Theophrastus Longuet is not at all flattered at having been *Car*—the *Child*. Give everyone his due. I should be much obliged if you'd put it that 'The *Child* went with his school-fellows.'"

"Certainly—certainly. At Saint-Laurent fair little Cartouche—"

"The *Child*!"

"But you weren't yet called the *Child*—you weren't called the *Child* till you were a man—"

"Well, say, 'Little Louis-Dominique.'"

"Louis-Dominique fell among a troop of gipsies—"

"That shows you that parents ought never to let their children go to fairs alone," said Theophrastus solemnly.

"The gipsies carried him off; they stole him—"

"Poor little Louis-Dominique: he deserves our pity," said Theophrastus in a tone of warm compassion. "Do they express pity for him in the books?"

"They say that he made no difficulties about being stolen."

"And what do they know about it!" cried Theophrastus indignantly.

"Well, the gipsies taught him cudgel-play, fencing, pistol-shooting, the art of springing from roof to roof, juggling, tumbling—"

"All very useful things," said Theophrastus in a tone of approval.

"They taught him to empty the pockets of tradesmen and gentlemen without their perceiving it. Oh, he was a nice boy! No one could touch him at collaring handkerchiefs, snuff-boxes, watches, sword-knots—"

"That was not at all nice!" cried Theophrastus in scandalised tones.

"Oh! If that were all!" said Adolphe gloomily. "The troop of gipsies was at Rouen, when Louis-Dominique fell ill."

"Poor little boy! He was never meant for such a life," cried Theophrastus compassionately.

"He was sent to the Rouen hospital; and there a brother of his father found him. He recognised him, embraced him with tears of joy, and swore to restore him to his parents."

"A fine fellow that uncle! Louis-Dominique was saved!" cried Theophrastus joyfully.

M. Lecamus lost patience, turned sharply on Theophrastus and begged him to cease his continual interruptions, declaring that it would take him a good ten years to tell the story of Cartouche, if he could not bring himself to listen without these comments.

"It's all very well for you to say that!" said Theophrastus with some heat. "But I should like to see *you* in my place! However, I'll do as you want; but just tell me first if Cartouche was as redoubtable as they say: was he a brigand chief?"

"He was indeed."

"Of many brigands?"

"At Paris alone he commanded about three thousand men."

"Three thousand? Goodness! That's a lot!"

"You had more than fifty lieutenants; and there were always about a city twenty men dressed exactly like you—in a reddish brown coat, lined with amaranthine silk, and wearing a patch of black cloth over the left eye—to put the police off your track."

"Oh, ho! it was a household of some size!" said Theophrastus, in a tone of irrepressible pride.

"They attribute to you more than a hundred and fifty murders by your own hand."

All this while Theophrastus had been trolling with a minnow without having had the slightest reason to suspect the existence of any fish in the waters of the Marne with the slightest appetite for his living bait. Of a sudden, the float which the minnow was drawing gently along among the green hearts of the water-lilies seemed smitten with frenzy. It leapt out of the water and plunged into it again, with such an unexpected swiftness and in such a resolute haste that it disappeared in the depths, carrying with it all the line which united it to the rod which united it to the hand of Theophrastus. The unfortunate thing was that after having taken after it all the line, it also took with it all the rod—with the result that nothing whatever united it any longer to the empty hand of Theophrastus.

"The blackguard!" cried Theophrastus, with a gesture of despair, in such a manner that it is impossible to say whether he used that strong expression, so rare in his mouth, about the murderer of the past or the fish of the present.

He added however: "It must have weighed a good four pounds!"

Taking everything into account, Theophrastus appeared to regret the loss of his fish more bitterly than his hundred and fifty murders.

Adolphe condoled with him and went on with his story.

"This good uncle," he said, "rescued little Cartouche from his wretched condition, took him from the Rouen hospital, and restored him to his parents. There was joy in Cabbage-Bridge Street—it was at number nine Cabbage-Bridge Street that little Cartouche was born and his father followed the trade of cooper. Louis-Dominique, warned by his early misfortunes, swore that for the future there should not be a more obedient son or steadier apprentice than he in all Paris. He helped his good father make casks; and it was a pleasure to see him ply the hammer and adze from early dawn to dewy eve. He seemed to be making it his first business to forget his disastrous truancy. The few months he had passed in the company of the gipsies had however been of some service to him in that they had taught him some of the arts of pleasing; and in the dinner hour he would amuse his fellow workmen by conjuring tricks, and on holidays there was a rush to invite his family to dinner in order that the company might be amused by his dexterity and humour. He was a great success in the neighbourhood; and his growing renown filled him with pride.

"In these occupations he reached that happy age at which the least sensible of human beings feels his beating heart awake the tenderest sentiments in him; and Louis-Dominique fell in love. The object of his affections was charming. She was a little milliner of Portefoin Street, with blue eyes, golden hair, a slender figure, and coquettish in the extreme—"

"But I see nothing wrong in all this," Theophrastus interrupted. "It's all very natural, and shows no signs of depravity whatever. How he turned out so badly passes my comprehension."

Adolphe looked at him gloomily and said, "I've just told you that the little milliner was a coquette. She was fond of dress and finery and trinkets, and burned to outshine her friends. Very soon the modest earnings of Louis-Dominique did not suffice to pay for her fancies—"

"Oh, these women!" cried Theophrastus, clenching his fists.

"You seem to forget that you have a wife who is your chief joy and pride," said Adolphe with some severity.

"That's true," said Theophrastus. "But you forget that I am as deeply interested in the adventures of the *Child* as if they were my own; and I am naturally irritated to see him so seriously compromise his future for the sake of a little milliner of Portefoin Street."

"Well, presently he robbed his father; and his father was not long finding it out. He obtained an Order of Committal by which he could make his son enter the Convent of the Lazarists of the Faubourg Saint-Denis, which was really a House of Correction."

"Just like parents!" said Theophrastus bitterly. "Instead of combating the evil instincts of their children by kindness, they drive them to despair by shutting them up in these villainous reformatories, where they only find bad examples, and where the spirit of revolt ferments, gathers force, boils over, and suffocates every other sentiment in their innocent young souls. I'd bet anything that if they had not shut up Louis-Dominique in a House of Correction, none of the rest would have followed!"

"You needn't worry about that," said Adolphe drily. "Louis-Dominique was not shut up in a House of Correction."

"How did that come about?" said Theophrastus in a less eloquent tone.

"His father did not inform him of his discovery of his thefts, but one Sunday morning he invited him to come for a stroll. Louis-Dominique went with him with pleasure, for he was in a very good temper and had put on his best clothes with the intention of taking his sweetheart to the Palais-Royal in the afternoon. But when his father took the way to the Faubourg Saint-Denis, Louis-Dominique began to prick up his ears. He knew that at the end of the Faubourg were the Lazarists; and he also knew that parents sometimes took their children to the Lazarists. However, he showed none of the distrust which sprang from his uneasy conscience; but when they came to the corner of Paradise Street, and the buildings of Saint-Lazare rose before them, it seemed to Louis-Dominique that his father wore a strained air; and he took an instant dislike to the neighbourhood. He lagged a little behind.

"When his father turned to look for him, Louis-Dominique had disappeared; and he was never to see him again."

"And quite right too!" cried Theophrastus hotly. "In his place I should have done exactly the same!"

"*But you were in his place*," said Adolphe.

"Ah, yes—yes—of course I was! I keep forgetting it," said Theophrastus with less heat.

"WELL, YOU WERE NEXT HEARD of in a disreputable house on the other side of the Seine. Your pretty manners were found pleasing by frequenters of the *Three Tuns* tavern at the corner of Rat Street. But since there was no credit on that side of the Seine, you were presently under the necessity of using the accomplishments you had learned from the gipsies and betook yourself to lightening the pockets of passers-by of everything that weighed them down: snuff-boxes, purses, handkerchiefs, bon-bon boxes, and patch-boxes.

"After a while you became the confederate of a rascal of the name Galichon, who had taken a great fancy to you. You married his wife's sister. Marriage became quite a habit of yours; for, when at the end of six months Galichon, his wife, and his wife's sister were condemned to the galleys, you married an uncommonly clever pickpocket of Bucherie Street, and with her pursued your trade in the Palais-Royal."

"Disgraceful!" cried Theophrastus, overwhelmed with shame.

"But presently you were blown upon, and compelled to put your cunning at the disposal of the recruiting sergeants. The method of recruiting in those days was quite simple: the recruiting sergeants, to whom one brought simple young fellows or ragged ne'er-do-wells without a home, made everybody drunk; and when they awoke next morning, sober, they found that they had enlisted; and off to the wars they had to go. You provided the recruiting sergeants with recruits at a fixed price. But you were caught in your own trap; for having brought two young fellows to a recruiting sergeant one evening, you made merry with them at a tavern called 'the Sweethearts of Montrueil,' and awoke next morning to find that you had signed on yourself, you were the recruiter recruited."

"Well, I don't complain of that," said Theophrastus. "I always had a taste for the army. Besides, if I signed on, it proves that I could write; and you can tell the historians so from me."

A clock at Esbly chimed half-past six, and warned them that it was time to go home to dinner.

Adolphe broke off his story and took his rod to pieces; and they started for home.

On the way Theophrastus said: "Tell me, Adolphe: what was I like? I'm curious to know. I was a fine man, wasn't I? Big and well made?"

"You are like that on the stage in that piece of Ennery's. But, as a matter of fact, you were, according to the poet Granval, a man who knew you well and chanted your glory—"

"My what?" cried Theophrastus.

"Your sanguinary glory—you were:

'Brown, dried-up, thin, and small, by courage great,
Reckless and brisk, robust, alert, adroit.'"

Theophrastus frowned as if he would have preferred a more romantic picture; then he said, "You haven't told me how you got hold of that portrait in the house in Guénégaud Street."

"It's a copy of a photograph by Nadar."

"But how on earth did Nadar take my photograph?" cried Theophrastus in extreme surprise.

"He took it from a wax mask which must have been very like you, since it was moulded from your face by the order of the Regent. Nadar photographed this mask on the 17th of January, 1859."

"And where is it to be found?" said Theophrastus eagerly.

"At the Château de Saint-Germain."

"I must see that mask!" cried Theophrastus, "I must see it and touch it! We will go to Saint-Germain to-morrow."

At that moment the smiling Marceline opened the door of Azure Waves Villa for them.

VIII

The Wax Mask

At this point I let Theophrastus once more take up the narrative.

"I had the strongest desire," he writes, "to see and touch that wax which had been moulded on my own skin; and this desire grew, if possible, stronger when Adolphe told me that the Château of Saint-Germain-en-Laye had contained the wax portrait of the famous Cartouche since the 25th of April, 1849. It had been presented to it by an Abbé Niallier, who had inherited it under the will of a Monsieur Richot, an Officer of the Household of Louis XVI, who had had it for many years. It was all the more valuable for having belonged to the Royal Family.

"This bust was moulded by a Florentine artist a few days before my execution. On it is a cap of wool or rough leather; and it is dressed in a coarse linen shirt covered with soot, and a waistcoat and a jacket of black camlet. But the most extraordinary thing about it is, that my hair and moustache were cut off after I was executed, and glued on to my mask! The portrait is enclosed in a large, deep, gilded frame, a very pretty piece of work. A sheet of Venetian glass protects the portrait; and one can still see on the frame faint traces of the arms of France.

"I asked Adolphe how he had obtained these exact details. He answered that they were the result of two days' work in the National Library.

"My hair! my moustache! my clothes! All as they were two hundred years ago! In spite of the horror with which the relics of a man who had committed so many crimes should have inspired me, I could hardly contain myself in my impatience to see and touch them. O mystery of Nature! Profound abyss of the soul! Giddy precipice of the heart! I, Theophrastus Longuet, whose name is the synonym of honour, I who was always afraid of bloodshed, I already *cherished* in my heart the relics of the greatest brigand in the world!

"When I recovered my senses after the sight of the portrait in Guénégaud Street, I was at first amazed not to find myself in a state of despair bitter enough to disgust me with life, and plunge me once more into the tomb. No: I did not dream of suppressing this envelope, with the face of an honest man, which in the twentieth century was labelled

'Theophrastus Longuet,' which enclosed and bore about the world the soul of Cartouche. Undoubtedly at the first moment of such a revelation the least I could do was to faint; and I did so. But instead of finding despair in my heart I found a great compassion, which not only drew tears from me for the misfortune of myself, Theophrastus, but also for Cartouche. I asked myself in fact which was having the best time of it, the honest Theophrastus dragging the brigand Cartouche about inside him or the brigand Cartouche shut up in the honest Theophrastus.

"'We must try and understand one another,' I said out loud.

"The words had scarcely passed my lips when a dazzling light broke on me, as I recalled the theory of Reincarnation which M. Lecamus had revealed to me.

"The whole object of evolution is the evolution of the reincarnate soul towards the Better. It is the Progressive Ascent of Being of which Commissary Mifroid had spoken to us with such delightful earnestness. It was quite plain that the powers who regulate the process of reincarnation had found nothing more honest on earth than the body of Theophrastus Longuet to enable the criminal soul of Cartouche to evolve towards the Better.

"I must admit that when this idea took hold of me, instead of the childish despair which had caused me to faint, I felt myself filled with a sentiment more akin to pride. I was charged by the Planetary Logos, I, the humble, honest Theophrastus, to regenerate in ideal splendour that soul of darkness and of blood, the soul of Louis-Dominique Cartouche, known as the *Child*. I accepted willingly, since I could not do otherwise, this unexpected mission and at once I was on my guard. I did not repeat the phrase, 'We must understand one another'; but I at once commanded Cartouche to obey Theophrastus; and I promised myself that I would give him such a time of it that I could not prevent myself from saying with a smile: 'Poor old Cartouche!'

"I confided these reflections to Adolphe, who received them with approval, but at the same time warned me against my tendency to separate Theophrastus from Cartouche.

"'You must not forget,' he said, 'that they are one. You have the instincts of Theophrastus, that is to say, of the cabbage-planters (gardeners, market-gardeners) of Ferté-sous-Jouarre. These instincts are good. But you have also the soul of Cartouche, which is detestable. Take care: war is declared. The question is, which will conquer, the soul of long ago or the instincts of to-day.'

"I asked him if the soul of Cartouche was truly altogether detestable, which would have grieved me. I was pleased to learn that it had its good points.

"'Cartouche,' said he, 'expressly forbade his men to kill, or even wound, wayfarers without some reason. When he was at work in Paris with any of his bands, and his men brought him prisoners, he spoke to them with the utmost politeness and gentleness and made them restore a part of their spoil. Sometimes the affair was confined to a mere exchange of clothes. When he found in the pockets of the coat thus exchanged letters of importance, he ran after its late owner to give them back to him, wished him a pleasant evening, and gave him the password. It was a maxim of this extraordinary man that no one ought to be robbed twice on the same night, or treated too harshly, in order that the Parisians might not take a dislike to going out in the evening.'

"Since, then, he was opposed to unreasonable murder, it is clear that this man was not utterly wicked. I regret, however, that, as far as he himself was concerned, he should have had in the course of his life a hundred and fifty reasons for assassinating his contemporaries.

"But to come back to the wax mask, my friend Adolphe and myself had just descended from the train at Saint-Germain station when I fancied that I saw among a group of passengers a figure which I knew. Moved by a sentiment which was not altogether under my control, I dashed towards the group, but the figure had disappeared.

"'That form is essentially repugnant to me. Where have I seen it?' said I to myself; and Adolphe asked me the reason of my excitement. All at once I remembered.

"'I could swear that it was Signor Petito, the Professor of Italian who lives in the flat above us!' I cried. 'What is Signor Petito up to at Saint-Germain? He had better not get in my way!'

"'What is it he's done?' said Adolphe, in some surprise at the emphasis with which I uttered the last sentence.

"'Oh, nothing—nothing. Only if he gets in my way I swear to you *I'll clip his ears for him*!'

"And I would have done as I said, you know.

"We went on then, without bothering any more about Signor Petito, to the Château, that wonderful Château. We went into the museum; and I was extremely annoyed to find that those chambers which knew the whole history of France, and would have served as the frame of our past, even had they been empty, should be serving to-day as a bazaar for Roman plaster casts, prehistoric arms, elephants' tusks, and bas-reliefs from the Arch of Constantine. But my annoyance turned to fury when I learnt that the mask of Cartouche was not there. I had just stealthily thrust the ferule of my green umbrella into the eye of a plaster legionary and smashed it, when an old custodian came to us and said that he was sure there was a mask of Cartouche at Saint-Germain and he thought it was in the library; but that had, for a week, been closed for repairs.

"We decided that we would return at a more favourable opportunity; for the further the mask withdrew itself, the fiercer I burned to touch it.

"We went out on to the terrace, for it was a glorious day, and plunged into the forest, down a magnificent aisle of it, which brought us to the lodges built in front of the Château by the desire of Queen Anne of Austria.

"As we reached the left corner of the wall, I thought I once more recognised, slinking into a thicket, the abominable silhouette and repulsive face of Signor Petito. Adolphe maintained that I was mistaken.

"Was it because I was treading this old soil which I knew, because I found myself in that friendly forest among those familiar trees, or was it the result of a long, suggestive conversation about old times and the people of long ago? Of a sudden memory sprang to birth in me, a very pleasant memory, as sometimes a moving remembrance of one's youthful days comes back to one, days which one believed for ever lost, buried in the memory. And then I saw quite clearly that I was *the same* soul, for I recalled Cartouche as if we had not been separated *by two hundred years of death*.

"Yes, I had the same soul, a long same soul indeed: at one end was Cartouche, at the other Theophrastus.

"I remembered the old days; and above all I remembered them when we had passed the northern wall, plunging always deeper into the forest. I threw myself down on the turf at the foot of an immemorial tree, my eyes sparkling with an amazing youthful fire, and looking round the spot I knew so well, I said:

"'Ah, Adolphe! the last time I was here my fortune was at its height. I was feared and loved by all. I was even loved, Adolphe, by my victims, I plundered them so gracefully that afterwards they went about Paris singing my praises. I was not yet a prey to that dreadful thirst for blood which was some months later to drive me to commit the most atrocious crimes. Everything went well with me, feared and loved by all, I was happy, light-hearted, of a splendid daring, magnificent in love, of the finest nature in the world, and *master of Paris*.

"'Do you remember that glorious September night when we broke into the house of the Ambassador of Spain, made our way into his wife's bedroom, took all her embroidered robes of silk and velvet, a buckle set with twenty-seven large diamonds (one might almost fancy that it happened yesterday), a necklace of fine pearls, six gold plates, six gold knives and forks, and ten silver-gilt goblets (what a thing what a wonderful thing, my dear Adolphe, the phenomenon of memory is!)? Do you remember how we wrapped up the jewels and plate in napkins, and went off to supper (oh, what an evening it was!) at La Belle Hélène's, who, *you remember*, kept the Heart tavern?

"Now why, I wonder, did I say '*You remember*'? It must be that I regard you as a friend I had in those days, as trusty as yourself, of whom I was just as fond—Old Easy-Going—my favourite friend. *By the throttle of Madame Phalaris!* he was a fine fellow—sergeant of the City Guard and one of my lieutenants. What a lot of those City Guards I did have among my men! Why, when I was arrested, *a hundred and fifty of them, officers and men, fled to the colonies* for fear I should split. They had no need to: torture never drew a word from me!

"'Do you remember the night you were on duty at the Palais-Royal and stole the Regent's silver-gilt candlesticks?'"

The voice of Theophrastus died dreamily away down the vistas of the past; but M. Adolphe Lecamus said nothing: his face was flushed; and he was breathing heavily.

Presently Theophrastus woke from his dream to tell his friend of yet another outrageous exploit, the theft of Mississippi Bonds to the value of a million and three hundred thousand francs from the great financier Law. He ended the story by saying, "How two hundred years do change a man!"

Then he began to laugh at the phrase. He was joking, positively joking. That is the way with the Parisian tradesman of to-day: he begins by being scared to death by a mere nothing, and ends by laughing at everything. Theophrastus Longuet had reached the point of laughing at himself. The preternatural and terrifying antithesis between Cartouche and Longuet, which had at first plunged him into the gloomiest terror, a few days later became a joke! The wretched man was insulting Destiny! He was mocking the thunder! His excuse is that he did not realise the gravity of his case.

Adolphe showed but little appreciation of his humour. At dusk they returned to Paris; and as they came out of Saint-Lazare station, he said to Theophrastus:

"Tell me, Theophrastus, when you're Cartouche and are walking about Paris and observing its life, what astonishes you most? Is it the telephone, or the railway, or the motorcars, or the Eiffel Tower?"

"No, no!" said Theophrastus quickly. "It's the policemen!"

IX

Strange Position of a Little Violet Cat

It would seem that the Destiny which rules mankind takes a detestable pleasure in making the most serene joys come before the worst catastrophes. Never had the three friends enjoyed a dinner more than the dinner which they had that night at the café Des Trois Etoiles. They dined well, the coffee was excellent, and the cigars which Adolphe had brought with him, and the Russian cigarettes which Marceline smoked, were excellent too. They lingered talking together for a long while after dinner; and their talk, which, under the guidance of Adolphe, never wandered far from the sphere of the occult which now so practically concerned them, was interesting and fascinating, in spite of the fact that that inveterate Parisian Theophrastus would now and again jest about his dangerous plight. At half-past ten they left the restaurant and walked back to the flat in Gerando Street. Adolphe bade them good-night at the bottom of the stairs.

That flat consisted of a narrow hall, nearly filled, and certainly cramped, by a chest of polished oak. Into this hall four doors opened, those of the kitchen and dining-room on the left, those of the drawing-room and bedroom, which looked out on to the street, on the right. There was a third window looking out on to the street, that of the tiny room which Theophrastus had made his study. *This study had two doors; one of them opened into the bedroom, the other into the dining-room.* In this study was a bureau against the wall; and in it were drawers above and below its writing-table. This writing-table let down and shut up, and was fastened by a somewhat elaborate lock at the edge of the bureau's top. When it was locked, all the drawers were locked too. As a rule, Theophrastus used to set a little violet cat on the keyhole of the lock, as much to hide it as for ornament.

This little violet cat, which had glass eyes, was nothing but an ingenious silk ball which acted as a pen-wiper and pin-cushion. About four feet away from the desk was a very small *tea-table*.

On entering their flat, Theophrastus and Marceline, as was their custom, made a careful search in every room for a hidden burglar. Having, as usual, failed to find one, (Heaven alone knows what they would have done with him if they had!) they went to bed with their minds at ease. As the more timid of the two, Theophrastus slept next the wall. They were soon asleep, Theophrastus snoring gently.

Night. Not a carriage in the street. Silence.

The snoring of Theophrastus ceased. Was it that he had sunk into a deeper sleep? No: he sleeps no more. His throat is dry; he stares into the darkness with affrighted eyes; he grips with a cold hand, a hand which fear is freezing, the shoulder of Marceline and awakens her.

He says in a low voice, so low that she does not even hear him, "Do you hear?"

Marceline holds her breath; she clutches her husband's icy hand. They strain their ears; and they undoubtedly do hear something—*in the flat*.

In very truth it is nothing to laugh at. The man who can laugh at an inexplicable noise, at night, *in a flat*, has not yet been born! There are brave men, splendidly brave, who will stick at nothing, who will go anywhere at night, into the emptiest streets of the most disreputable quarters, who would not hesitate to venture, just for the pleasure of it, into lampless blind alleys. But I tell you, because it is the truth, and you know it is the truth, that the man who can laugh at an inexplicable noise, at night, *in a flat*, has not yet been born.

We have already seen Theophrastus sleepless on the night of the revelation of the dreadful secret which sprang from the stones of the Conciergerie. The anxiety which weighed on his heart that night, terrible as it had been, was as nothing compared with that which was now strangling him, because there was at night, *in the flat*, an inexplicable noise.

It was truly an odd noise, but beyond all doubting real; it was a long-drawn *pur-r-r-r-r-r-r-r-r-r*. It came from behind the wall of the next room.

They sat up in bed noiselessly, with bristling hair, and beads of cold sweat standing out on their brows. From the other side of the wall came the strange *pur-r-r-r-r-r-r-r-r*. It was the purring of a cat; they recognised that purring: it was the purring of the little violet cat. Marceline slipped down under the clothes and whispered:

"It's the purring of the violet cat. Go and see what's the matter with it, Theophrastus."

Theophrastus did not budge; he would have given a hundred thousand rubber stamps to be walking along the boulevard at mid-day.

"It's not natural that it should be purring like that," she added. "Go and see what's the matter with it. You must, Theophrastus! Get your revolver out of the drawer."

Theophrastus found the strength to say faintly, "You know quite well that it's not loaded."

They listened again; the purring had ceased; Marceline began to hope they had been mistaken. Then Theophrastus groaned, got out of bed, took the revolver, and quietly opened the door leading into his study. It was bright in a sheet of moonlight; and what Theophrastus saw made him recoil with a dull cry, shut the door, and set his back against it as if to bar what he saw from entering the bedroom.

"What is it?" said Marceline hoarsely.

The teeth of Theophrastus chattered as he said, "It has stopped purring; but it has moved!"

"Where is it?"

"On the tea-table."

"The violet cat is on the tea-table?"

"Yes."

"Are you quite sure it was in its place last night?"

"Quite sure. I stuck my scarf-pin in its head. It was on the bureau, as it always is."

"You must have imagined it. Suppose I lit the light?" said Marceline.

"No, no, we might escape in the darkness. . . Suppose I went and opened the door on to the landing, and called the porter?"

"Don't get so terrified," said Marceline, who was little by little recovering her wits, since she no longer heard the violet cat. "The whole thing was an illusion. You changed its place last night; and it didn't purr."

"After all, it's quite possible," said Theophrastus, whose one desire was to get back into bed.

"Go and put it back in its place," said Marceline.

Theophrastus braced himself to the effort, went into the study, and with a swift and trembling hand took the cat from the tea-table, set it back on the bureau, and hurried back into bed.

The violet cat was no sooner back on the bureau than he began again his *pur-r-r-r-r-r-r*. That purring only made them smile: they knew what had set it going. A quarter of an hour had passed; they were almost asleep, when a second fright made them spring up in bed. A third purring struck on their ears. If the first purring had smitten them with terror, and the second made them smile, the third purring frightened them out of their lives.

"It's impossible!" said Marceline in a chattering whisper. "We're victims of an hallucination! B-B-B-Besides, it's n-n-not really surprising after what happened to you at the Conciergerie!"

The purring once more ceased. This time it was Marceline who rose. She opened the door of the study, turned sharply towards Theophrastus, and said, but in what a faint and dying voice:

"You didn't put the violet cat back on the bureau!"

"But I did!" groaned Theophrastus.

"*But it's gone back to the tea-table!*"

"Good God!" cried poor Theophrastus; and he buried his head under the bed-clothes.

The violet cat no longer purred. Marceline became persuaded that in his perturbation her husband had left it on the tea-table. She took it up, holding her breath, and set it back on the bureau. The violet cat made its purring heard for the fourth time. Marceline and Theophrastus heard it with the same equanimity with which they had heard the second purring. The fourth purring stopped.

Another quarter of an hour passed: they were not asleep or even sleepy; and then there came *a fifth purring*.

Then, incredible to relate, Theophrastus leapt from the bed like a tiger, and cried:

"*By the throttle of Madame Phalaris!* This is too much of a good thing! What the deuce is that infernal violet cat up to?"

X

The Explanation of the Strange Attitude of a Little Violet Cat

It is necessary to mount to the floor above, to the flat occupied by Signor and Signora Petito, to the room in which Theophrastus, with never a thought of the imprudence he was committing, had asked for the needful information about the handwriting of the document. What imprudence indeed could there be in showing to an expert in handwriting a document so torn, stained, and obliterated that it was impossible, at a first glance, to discover any sense or meaning at all in it?

Yet by a truly strange chance it was that very document that Signor Petito and his wife were that night discussing.

The Signora Petito was saying: "I don't understand it at all; and the behaviour of M. Longuet at Saint-Germain throws no fresh light on it. The fact is, you do not remember the instructions—all the instructions. *Go and take the air at the Chopinettes, look at the Cock, look at the Gall*: it's all so vague. What can it mean?"

"The first thing it means is that the treasure is to be found on the outskirts of Paris, of the Paris of that epoch. *Go and take the air. . .* My opinion is that we ought to search in the neighbourhood of Montrouge, or Montmartre, because of the Cock. There was a Château du Coq at Porkers village. Look at this plan of old Paris," said her husband.

They pored over the plan on the table.

"It's still very vague," said Signor Petito gloomily. "For my part, I think we ought to pay particular attention to the words 'The Gall.'"

"That's just the vaguest thing in the whole thing," said his wife.

"Still, I'm sure it's important," said her husband. "As I remember the document (and you know what a magnificent memory I have), there was a short space between the word 'the' and the word 'Gall,' and after 'Gall' a longer space. Reach me the dictionary."

The Signora Petito rose with the greatest precaution, she walked noiselessly and stealthily across the room (she was the conspirator to her finger-tips), and brought a small dictionary. They began to run down a column, writing down all the words which began with the syllable gall: Gallantly, Gallery, Galley, and so forth. Then the clock on the mantelpiece began to strike twelve.

The Signora Petito paled and rose to her feet; Signor Petito rose to his feet paler still.

"The hour has come!" said the Signora Petito. "You will find the information you want below." She pointed a rigid finger at the floor. "They cannot hear you in your list slippers. Besides, there's no danger of it: they are at Esbly."

Two minutes later a dark figure glided down to M. Longuet's flat, slipped a key into the lock of his door, and entered his hall. The flat of Theophrastus was of exactly the same construction as that of Signor Petito, and he found his way into the dining-room without a pause. He acted with the greater coolness because he believed that the flat was empty. He opened the door of the study, and saw the violet cat on the bureau. Since it was evidently on the lock of the bureau in which he was interested, he took it up, and set it on the tea-table. Then he hurried noiselessly back through the dining-room into the hall, for he fancied he heard voices on the staircase.

He listened for a while at the door of the flat and heard nothing; doubtless his ears had deceived him. Then he came back to the study. He found *the violet cat on the bureau, purring*.

In spite of their crinkliness, the hairs of Signor Petito stood stiffly upright on his head, the horror which filled him can only be compared to that other horror on the other side of the wall.

He stood motionless, panting, in the moonlight, even after the little violet cat had stopped purring. Then he braced himself, and with a timid hand picked up the violet cat. As soon as he had moved it, it began to purr; and he became acquainted with the fact that in its cardboard interior there was a small marble which, as it rolled to and fro, produced an ingenious imitation of a natural purr. Since he had been frightened to death, he called himself a perfect fool. It was all quite clear; had he not before slipping out of the study moved the cat? Instead of having set it on the tea-table, as he thought, he had put it back on the bureau. Of course, it was quite simple. He set it back, still purring, on the tea-table.

It must not be forgotten that this purring, which did not terrify Signor Petito, terrified Theophrastus and his wife afresh, while the second purring, which had taken the curl out of Signor Petito's hair with terror, had not terrified them at all.

The cat was still purring, when there was another noise outside the flat. It was Signora Petito sneezing in the draught. Signor Petito hurried back into the hall and once more glued his ear to the door of the flat. When, reassured, he returned to the study, *the purring violet cat had gone back to the bureau*.

He thought he was going to die of fright; he thought that a miraculous intervention was holding him back on the verge of a crime. He uttered a swift prayer in which he assured Heaven that he would not go on with it. However a quarter of an hour passed in the recovery of his scattered wits; and since he heard nothing more, he attributed these surprising happenings to the perturbation of spirit induced by his exceptional occupation. He took up the violet cat, which began to purr again.

But this time the door of the study was flung violently open; and Signor Petito fell swooning into the arms of M. Longuet, *who expressed no surprise whatever*.

M. Longuet contemptuously flung Signor Petito on the floor, dashed at the violet cat, caught it up, opened the window, tore his scarf-pin out of its head, and threw it into the street.

"You beastly cat!" he cried with inexpressible fury. "You'll never stop our sleeping again!"

Signor Petito had dragged himself to his feet, entirely at a loss to know what face to put upon the matter, inasmuch as Madame Longuet, in her nightgown, was assiduously pointing at him a large, shining, nickel-plated revolver. He only found the phrase:

"I beg your pardon: *I thought you were in the country*."

But it was M. Longuet who came to him, took between his thumb and first finger one of Signor Petito's long ears, and said:

"And now, *my dear Signor Petito, we are going to have a little talk*!"

Marceline lowered the barrel of the revolver; and at the sight of his calm courage, gazed at her husband in an ecstasy of admiration.

"You see, my dear Signor Petito, I am calm," said Theophrastus. "Just now, indeed, I was in a devil of a temper, but that was against that infernal cat which prevented us from sleeping. So I threw it out of the window. But cheer up, Signor Petito, I am not going to throw you out of the window. Mine is a just nature. It wasn't you who prevented us from sleeping. You have taken the precaution of putting on list slippers. Many thanks for it. Why then, my dear Signor Petito, are you making that intolerable face? Of course, it must be your ear. I've good news for you then, news which will set you quite at your ease about your ear: *You are not going to suffer from your ears any longer*, my dear Signor Petito!"

Then he bade his wife put on a dressing-gown, and begged Signor Petito come into the kitchen.

"Don't be surprised at my receiving you in my kitchen," he said. "*I am very careful of my carpets, and you will bleed like a pig.*"

He dragged a table of white wood from against the wall to the middle of the kitchen, and bade Marceline spread a piece of oil-cloth on it, and fetch him the big bowl, and the carving-knife from the drawer of the dining-room sideboard.

Marceline tried to ask for an explanation; but her husband gave her such a look that she could only shiver and obey. Signor Petito shivered too, and as he shivered, he made for the door of the kitchen, in which, he told himself, there was nothing for him to do. M. Longuet, unfortunately, refused absolutely to let his neighbour go. He bade him sit down, and sat down himself.

"Signor Petito," he said in a tone of the most exquisite politeness, "I do not like your face. It is not your fault; but it is certainly not mine. There is no doubt that you are the most cowardly and contemptible of sneak-thieves. But what of that? It's no business of mine, but of some honest executioner of the King who will invite you next season *to go harvesting at the ladder*, where one fine day he will set you *floating gently in the breeze* to the end that, like a fine fellow, *you may keep the sheep of the moon*. Don't smile, Signor Petito." Signor Petito was not smiling. "You have absurd ears; and I am certain that with ears like those you never dare go near Guilleri Cross-roads."

Signor Petito clasped his hands and said with chattering teeth, "My wife's waiting for me."

"What are you doing, Marceline?" cried Theophrastus impatiently. "Can't you see that Signor Petito is in a hurry? His wife's waiting for him! *Have you got the carving-knife?*"

"I can't find the fork," replied the trembling voice of Marceline.

The fact is, Marceline did not know what she was saying. She thought that her husband had gone quite mad; and between Signor Petito burglar, and Theophrastus mad, she was not in the mood for joking. She had instinctively hidden herself behind a cupboard door; and such was her agitation that in turning a little clumsily, at the moment at which Theophrastus was bellowing a volley of abuse at her, she upset the dessert service, and the Sarreguemines vase which was its chief ornament. The result was a loud crash and the utmost confusion. Theophrastus appealed once more to the throttle of Madame Phalaris and called Marceline to him in such a furious roar that in spite of herself she ran into the kitchen. A dreadful sight awaited her.

The eyes of Signor Petito seemed to be starting from their sockets. Was it from fear? Fear had something to do with it, but also the suffocation produced by the handkerchief which Theophrastus had thrust into his mouth. Signor Petito himself lay at full length on the table. Theophrastus had had the time and strength to bind his wrists and ankles with string. The Signor's head projected a little beyond the table's edge; and under his head was a bowl which M. Longuet had placed there *not to make a mess*. Theophrastus himself with twitching nostrils (that was what Marceline chiefly noticed in the terrifying face of her husband) had hold of Signor Petito's right ear with the fingers of his left hand, and his right hand gripped a kitchen knife. He ground his teeth and said:

"*Strike the flag!*"

With these words he sliced neatly off Signor Petito's left ear.

He dropped the ear into a little basin which he had ready, caught hold of the right ear, sliced off that, then carried the little basin to the sink, and turned on the tap.

He returned to the kitchen; and while he waited for Signor Petito's ears to stop bleeding, hummed an old and forgotten French air, with the most cheerful face in the world. When the bleeding ceased, he fastened a dish-cloth round Signor Petito's head, withdrew the handkerchief from his mouth, cut the string which bound him, and bade him get out of his flat at once if he did not wish to be arrested for burglary.

As the groaning expert in handwriting was leaving the kitchen, Theophrastus bethought himself, rushed to the sink, took the ears out of the basin, and slipped them into their owner's waistcoat pocket.

"You go about forgetting everything!" he said indignantly. "What would the Signora Petito think, if you came home without your ears?"

XI

Theophrastus Maintains that He did not Die on the Place de Grève

In his account, in his Memoirs, of that terrible night, M. Longuet appears to attach very little importance to clipping the ears of Signor Petito. He seems far more deeply concerned with the psychology of Mme. Longuet. "The soul of woman," he writes, "is a very delicate thing. I gathered this from the emotion of my dear Marceline. She would not admit that I was obliged to clip the ears of Signor Petito; and her process of reasoning was incredible and indeed incomprehensible. But I forgave her on account of her excessive sensitiveness. She said then that I was not obliged to clip Signor Petito's ears. I answered that manifestly one was never obliged to clip any man's ears any more than one was obliged to kill him; and yet, ninety-nine men out of a hundred, I affirmed (and no one will contradict me) would have killed Signor Petito when they found him in their flat at night. She herself, who was after all only a woman, would have done all she could to kill Signor Petito with the revolver in her hand, had it been loaded. She did not deny it. Well then, in clipping his ears, did I not demonstrate that there was no need to kill him?

"A man prefers to live earless rather than die with his ears on; and Signor Petito found himself as thoroughly disgusted with night excursions into other people's flats as if he had been killed.

"I acted for the best with great restraint and inconceivable humanity.

"The logic of this reasoning calmed her a little; and what was left of the night would have passed comfortably, if I had not taken it into my head to reveal to her the whole mystery of my personality. It was her own fault. She insisted on knowing the reason of my sudden courage: which was natural enough, since up to that day I had hardly been a man of courage. It is not in selling rubber stamps that one learns to see the blood flow. Thereupon I told her straight off that I was Cartouche; and in a boastful vein which surprised me, I bragged of my hundred and fifty murders. She sprang out of bed, with every sign of extreme terror, took refuge behind the sofa, and informed me that she would have nothing more to do with Cartouche and was going to divorce me. On hearing this, I was deeply moved and began to weep. At this she came a little nearer, and explained how difficult her position was, when she had believed herself married to an honest man, and all at once discovered that she was the wife of a horrible brigand; that henceforth there could be no peace for her. I dried my tears, and condoled with her on her misfortune. We resolved to consult Adolphe.

"Adolphe came early next morning and had a long interview with Marceline in the drawing-room. When they came out, Adolphe regarded me sadly, asked me to go with him, for he had some shopping to do; and we strolled down into Paris. On the way I asked him if the study of the document had revealed any new fact concerning our treasures; and he answered that all that could wait, that my health was the first consideration, and we would all three take the evening train to Azure Waves Villa.

"I turned the talk on to the subject of Cartouche; but he shrank from it, until I was on the point of losing my temper at his reticence. Then he began to talk about it, and presently warmed to the subject. He took up my story at the point of my enlistment, and informed me that at the end of the war the greater part of the troops were disbanded, and that I found myself in Paris without any resources save those of my natural ingenuity and my special accomplishments. I employed these with such fortune and address that my comrades lost no time in electing me chief; and since we were successful, our band very quickly increased in numbers.

"Now, at that time, the Police of Paris was in such a wretched state that I resolved to make it my business. It was my intention that everyone, gentleman, tradesman, or churchman, should be able to walk at any hour in all tranquillity about the good city of Paris. I divided up my troops very skilfully, appointed a district to each, and a leader who would remain my obedient lieutenant. When anyone went abroad after the Curfew or even before it, he was accosted politely by a squad of my men, and invited to pay up a certain sum, or if he had no money on him, to part with his coat. In return for this he was furnished with the password, and could afterwards walk about Paris, all night long if he wished, in perfect security, for I had become the chief of all the robbers.

"I should be unworthy of the name of man, if I shrank from admitting that, to my shame, I admired myself for having risen to such a prodigious height of criminal enterprise. Quite criminal, alas! for though my intention of policing Paris might have been an admirable idea in itself, its execution drew us on to excesses that the original good faith of the plan could not excuse. The tradesfolk did not understand, and often resisted; and their resistance produced disaster. The clergy, however, were not against us, since we respected the churches. Indeed an unfrocked priest, whom we called the Ratlet, rendered us some services which presently led him to pronounce the Benediction with his feet in the air, *in communi patibulo*.

"Here I stopped Adolphe, to ask the meaning of the Latin words. He said that if I had really been a fellow-pupil of Voltaire at Clermont College I ought to know Latin, and that *in communi patibulo* meant 'on the common gibbet.'

"'Ah! I know: we often passed it when we went to have a blow-out at Chopinettes mill,' said I.

"'Oh, there were plenty of gibbets,' answered Adolphe, giving me a look of which I did not catch the meaning. 'The good city was not lacking in gibbets, gallows, or pillories. And even here. . .'

"Again he gave me an odd look, and I saw that we had arrived at the Place de l'Hôtel-de-Ville. 'Do you want to cross the Place de l'Hôtel-de-Ville?' he went on.

"'Of course I'll cross it, if that's the way you want to go,' I said.

"'Have you often crossed it?' he said.

"'Thousands of times.'

"'And has nothing uncommon happened? Have you experienced no odd feelings? Have you remembered nothing?'

"'Nothing at all.'

"'Are there any spots in Paris that you haven't been able to cross?'

"His look was insistent. It seemed to speak to me, to bid me reflect. Then I recalled several inexplicable aversions to places I had felt. More than once, on my way to Odéon Street, on finding myself in front of the Institute, I had turned into Mazarine Street. I had no sooner set foot in it than I had turned right about face and gone round another way. I had been vaguely aware of these changes of route and had put them down to absent-mindedness. But the more I think of it the less I believe that it was anything of the kind. In fact, I have found myself at that point more than twenty times; and more than twenty times I have retraced my steps. Never—never have I walked along that part of Mazarine Street which begins at the Institute and continues to the corner of Guénégaud Street and to the foot of the Pont-Neuf. Never! At the same time when I have gone along Mazarine Street on my way to the quays, I have stopped at Guénégaud Street and gone down it with a sense of pleasure.

"I told Adolphe all this; and he said, 'Are there any other places from which you shrink?'

"Then I remembered on reflection that I had never crossed the Pont-Neuf or the Petit-Pont; and that there is, at the corner of Vielle-du-Temple Street, a house with barred windows from which I have always recoiled.

"'And why do you shrink from these places and from this house in Vielle-du-Temple Street?' he said.

"Then I remembered exactly why; and the reason is the most natural in the world. I had thought I had no reason; but evidently I had, for it was because of the paving-stones.

"'Because of the paving-stones?' he said in a tone of surprise.

"'Yes: because the paving-stones in those streets are red. I don't mind red roofs or red-brick walls, but red paving-stones I cannot stand!'

"'And the soil of this Place de l'Hôtel-de-Ville? Isn't it red?' said Adolphe, leaning over me with the air of a doctor listening to the beating of a patient's heart.

"'Do you think I'm colour-blind?'

"'Don't you know that this was the Place de Grève?'

"'Zounds! It was here that the gibbet stood—and the pillory, and the platform on which the wheel was set up! On the days of execution! Facing the entrance of Vannerie Street! I never crossed this Place without saying to my comrades, to the Burgundian, Fancy Man, Gastelard, and Sheep's-head, "*We must avoid the wheel.*" And a lot of use it was to them!'

"'*Nor to you, either!*' retorted Adolphe. 'It was here that you were executed! It was here that you were broken on the wheel!'

"I burst out laughing in his face.

"'Who told you that piece of idiocy?' I said indignantly.

"'All the historians are agreed. . .'

"'The silly idiots! I know perfectly well that I died at the Gallows of Montfaucon!' I said with absolute assurance.

"'You? You died at the Gallows of Montfaucon?' cried Adolphe beside himself. 'You died in 1721 at the Gallows of Montfaucon? But it was years since they had executed anyone there!'

"But I protested still louder than he, so that we became the centre of a little crowd.

"'I didn't say that I was hanged at Montfaucon! the Gallows of Montfaucon! I said that I died there!' I cried.

"As I shouted it, I must have seemed to call to witness the truth of my words the forty persons who seemed interested in our altercation, of which indeed they can have understood nothing, with the exception of one gentleman who seemed to have caught its meaning, for he said to Adolphe with the utmost calmness, and with extreme politeness:

"'*Surely you're not going to teach this gentleman how he died!*'

"Adolphe admitted himself worsted; and we walked along arm in arm towards the Pont-Neuf."

XII

The House of Strange Words

Among all the papers I found in the sandalwood box, by Theophrastus himself, by M. Lecamus, or by Commissary Mifroid, those which relate to the death of Cartouche are beyond doubt the most curious and the most interesting. They are indeed of great historical interest since they contradict history. Moreover they contradict it with such force and with such irrefutable reasoning that one asks how men of such weight as Barbier, who was in the best position of all not to be duped, since he lived at the time, could have been the victims of a very poor comedy, and how succeeding generations have failed to suspect the truth.

History then, serious history, teaches us that Cartouche, after having undergone the Question in its cruellest form without revealing one single name or fact,—how Cartouche, who had only to die and nothing to hope, was brought to the Place de Grève to be executed, and that there he decided to confess; that they took him to the Hôtel-de-Ville, and that he delivered to justice his chief accomplices; after which he was broken on the wheel.

The papers of Theophrastus Longuet explain the fraud. Cartouche was not only an object of terror, but also an object of admiration. His courage knew no limits; and he proved it under torture. From the moment that the pain of the Boot failed to make him speak, it was morally impossible that he should speak. Why should he have spoken? All that was left for him was to die game. The greatest ladies of the Court and the city had hired boxes and windows to witness his execution. Among the three hundred and sixty people who were arrested were men whom he loved as brothers, and his tenderest and most constant flames. Some of them came to Paris from the Provinces, contemptuous of all danger, in the hope that, at the trial, the *Child* would have the consolation of seeing them for the last time. The account of the trial which describes these women as throwing themselves, after he had denounced them, into his arms at the Hôtel-de-Ville itself, is manifestly nonsense.

I will not reproduce here all the protests of M. Longuet against the dishonourable death ascribed to Cartouche, but the few lines which precede this chapter seem, to me at any rate, to prove, *a priori*, that he is right.

But at this moment all that M. Longuet knew was that *he died at the Gallows of Montfaucon, but that he was not hanged there*.

In the course of discussing this serious question Theophrastus and his friend had reached Petit-Pont Street without having crossed the Petit-Pont. Theophrastus did not so much as look in the direction of the Petit-Pont. Half-way down the street Theophrastus, who was in a state half of memory, half of possession, said to his friend: "Look at that house next to the hotel there, 'The Market-Gardeners' Hotel.' Do you notice anything remarkable about it?"

Adolphe looked across the street at the hotel, a little old house, low, narrow, and dirty, with "The Market-Gardeners' Hotel" newly painted on it. It seemed to be propping itself up against a large eighteenth-century building to which Theophrastus was pointing with his green umbrella. This building had a bulging balcony of wrought iron, of solid but delicate design.

"I see a very fine balcony," said Adolphe.

"What else?"

"The quiver of Cupid carved above the door."

"What else?"

"Nothing else."

"Don't you perceive the thick bars across the windows?"

"Of course I do."

"At that time, my dear Adolphe, people took the greatest care to have their windows barred; never did one see as many barred windows in Paris as in the year 1720. And I could swear that these bars here were fixed the day after the affairs of Petits-Augustins Street. First the Parisians garnished all their ground-floors with bars. But this precaution gave us no trouble at all since we had *Simon the Auvergnat*."

Adolphe thought the moment opportune to find out who Simon the Auvergnat, who was always appearing in their talk without any appreciable reason, exactly was.

"He was a very useful object, he was *the base of my column*," said Theophrastus.

"And what's that—the base of your column?"

"You don't understand? I'll just show you. Suppose you're Simon the Auvergnat," said Theophrastus with almost boyish eagerness.

Adolphe was quite willing, but not for long. Theophrastus drew him across the road, set him against the wall of the Market-Gardeners' Hotel, showed him the position he was to take: to set his legs apart, and lean, lowering his head and raising his crossed arms, against the wall.

"I place you here," he said, "because of the little ledge on the left, *I remember that it is very convenient*."

"And next?" said Adolphe, leaning against the wall in the required position.

"Next, since you are the base of my column, I mount on that base. . ."

Before M. Lecamus had the time so much as to imagine a movement even, Theophrastus had climbed up on to his shoulders, sprung on to the ledge, leapt from it with one bound to the balcony of the house next door, and vanished through an open window into the room which opened on to it. M. Lecamus in a dazed consternation was gazing into the air, and asked himself where his friend Theophrastus could have vanished, when the street rang with piercing cries. A despairing voice howled, "Help! thieves! murderers!"

"I might have expected it!" cried M. Lecamus; and he dashed into the house from which the screams issued, while the passers-by stood still, or hurried to the spot. He bounded up the great staircase with the swiftness of a young man, and reached the first floor at the very moment when a door opened, and Theophrastus appeared, hat in hand.

He was bowing low to an old lady with chattering teeth, and crowned with curl papers, and said:

"My dear madame, if I had thought for an instant that I should give you such a shock by entering your drawing-room by the window, I should have stayed quietly in the street. I am not, my dear madame, either a thief or a murderer, but an honest manufacturer of rubber stamps."

Adolphe seized his arm and tried to drag him down the stairs.

But Theophrastus went on: "It is entirely Adolphe's fault, my dear madame. He would have me show him how *Simon the Auvergnat acted as the base of my column*."

Adolphe, behind Theophrastus, made signs to the lady of the curl papers that his friend was off his head. Thereupon the lady fell fainting into the arms of her maid, who came running up. Adolphe dragged Theophrastus down the staircase just as the hall filled with people from the street. The crowd took them for fellow-rescuers; and they escaped from the house without difficulty.

In the street Theophrastus said cheerfully, "The most surprising thing about the whole matter, my dear Adolphe, was that this Simon the Auvergnat served us as the base of our column for more than two years without ever suspecting anything. He thought that he lent his strong shoulders to a band of young gentlemen of quality, who were amusing themselves!"

But Adolphe was not listening to Theophrastus. With one hand he was dragging him towards Huchette Street, and with the other he was wiping the sweat from his brow.

"The time has come!" he muttered. "The time has come!"

"Where are you dragging me to?" said Theophrastus.

"To see one of my friends," said Adolphe shortly, continuing to drag him along.

In Huchette Street they passed through a red porch into a very old house. Adolphe seemed to know his whereabouts, for he dragged Theophrastus up a dozen worn stone steps and pushed open a heavy door. They found themselves in a large hall, lighted by a lamp hanging by iron chains from the stone ceiling.

"Wait for me here, I shan't be long," said Adolphe, closing the door.

Theophrastus sat down in a large armchair, and gazed round him. The sight of the walls filled him with the wildest amazement. In the first place, there was an incredible quantity of words painted in black letters. They seemed to crawl about the wall without any order, like flies.

He spelt some of them to himself: Thabethnah, Jakin, Bohaz, Theba, Pic de la Mirandole, Paracelsus, Jacque Molay, Nephesch-Ruach-Neschamah, Ezechiel, Aïsha, Puysegur, Cagliostro, Wronski, Fabre d'Olivet, Louis Lucas, Hiram, Elias, Plotinus, Origen, Gutman, Swedenborg, Giorgius, Apollonius of Tyana, Cassidorus, Eliphas Levi, Cardan, Allan Kardec, Olympicodorus, Spinoza, and scores besides; and, repeated a hundred times, the word Ihoah. Turning towards the other wall, he saw a sphinx and the Pyramids, a huge rose, in the centre of which Christ stretched out his arms in a circle of flame, and these words on the rose: *Amphitheatrum sapientiæ æternæ solius veræ*. It was the rose of the Rosicrucians.

Below it were these words:

"Of what use are brands, and torches, and spectacles
To him who shuts his eyes that he may not see?"

"I am not shutting my eyes," said Theophrastus to himself, "and I am wearing spectacles, yet I'll be hanged if I know where I am!"

His eyes fell on this inscription in letters of gold:

"From the moment that you have performed an action, a single action, apply to it all the intelligence you have, seek its salient points, examine it in the light, *abandon yourself to hypotheses, fly in front of them, if need be*."

He saw hawks, vultures, jackals, men with heads of birds, several scarabs, a god with an ass's head, then a sceptre, an ass, and an eye.

Finally he read these words in blue letters:

"The more the soul shall be rooted in its instincts, the more it shall lie forgotten in the flesh, the less shall it have knowledge of its immortal life, *and the longer it shall remain prisoner in living carcasses*."

Growing impatient at the long absence of Adolphe, after a while he rose to draw apart the curtains through which his friend had disappeared. As he was about to pass through them, his head struck against two feet hanging in the air which rattled with the noise of dry bones. He looked up: it was a skeleton.

He gazed at it with a sincere and gentle compassion.

"You would be much more at your ease in Saint-Chaumont Cemetery," he said and went on with a sad smile.

The corridor down which he walked had no windows. It was lighted from one end to the other by a crimson glow. At first Theophrastus could not make out where it came from. Then he perceived that he was walking on it. It came from the cellars, through the thick sheets of glass with which the corridor was paved. What were those crimson flames below, in whose glow he walked, doing?

He did not know. He did not even ask. He did not even ask why he, Theophrastus, found himself walking in this glow. He had ceased to ask, "Why am I in this house in Huchette Street?" He had ceased to ask because nobody answered.

Emmanuel, Noun, Samech, Hain. . . Sabaoth. . . Adonai. . .

Still names on the stone walls.

The only ornament on these walls about which names crawled was, at the height of a man, an endless line of stars formed by the two triangles of Solomon's Seal. Between each star or seal, in green letters, was the word NIRVANA.

The corridor did not run in a straight line. It had curves and angles. Presently he came to a spot at which two other corridors ran into it at right angles, and prudently stopped. But soon he grew impatient again, and plunged down one of these side corridors. Three minutes later, without knowing how it came about, he found himself back at the spot where the corridors crossed. Then he went back down the first corridor, retracing his steps to the hall. But he did not find the hall.

He was on the point of howling with distress, when Adolphe appeared before him. His eyes were red as if he had been weeping.

"Where am I?" cried Theophrastus tempestuously.

"You are in the house of the Mage—in the house of M. Eliphas de Saint-Elme de Taillebourg de la Nox!"

XIII

The Cure that Missed

At hearing that he was at the house of M. Eliphas de Saint-Elme de Taillebourg de la Nox, Theophrastus was somewhat reassured, for he had heard both Marceline and Adolphe speak of him with reverence as a leading member of the Pneumatic Club. Theophrastus had chanced to hear of the Pneumatic Club; and he had caused Marceline to become a member of it (he was at the time too busy to join it himself) under the impression that it was the chief social club of the most prominent people in the Rubber Industry. But of course everybody knows that Pneumatology is that part of metaphysics which deals with the soul, in Greek *Pneuma*; and the Pneumatics are those versed in this science, which has nothing whatever to do with the elastic and resilient substance extracted by incision from a tree, which was named by the benighted savages who discovered it, the Caoutchouc. Marceline did not trouble the busy Theophrastus with her discovery that the Pneumatic Club was a branch of Spiritualism and not of the Rubber Industry. She contented herself with inviting M. Adolphe Lecamus to join it also; and both of them became devout admirers and disciples of that great expert in the Occult, M. Eliphas de Saint-Elme de Taillebourg de la Nox. It is no wonder that, on learning from Marceline of the painful affair of the ears of Signor Petito, M. Lecamus should have urged instant recourse to that great expert, to learn the proper methods of dealing with a reincarnate soul of such unfortunate antecedents.

Adolphe looked at Theophrastus with deep commiseration in his eyes, as if his conversation with the Mage had given him reason for dismay.

"Come along, Marceline is here; and we are going to introduce you to a good friend," he said sombrely.

He led the way down the corridor, opened a door, and ushered Theophrastus into a large, dim room. At once his eyes were attracted by a marvellous light which fell on the noblest, gentlest, and most beautiful face of a man he had ever seen. The light was marvellous because that striking figure did not seem to receive it, but to diffuse it. When it moved, the light moved with it; it was a figure and a torch. Before this torch knelt Marceline, her hands joined as if in supplication; and on her fell some of the rays from this gracious, almost divine figure.

Then Theophrastus heard a friendly voice, a male voice, but sweeter far than the voice of any woman, which said, "Come to me without fear."

Theophrastus still gazed in wonder at the kind of astral light which was diffused from the figure of the Mage, the light which the painter James Tissot has succeeded in reproducing, in an engraving of great beauty, from a photograph of a mediumistic apparition communicated to the Congress of Spiritualists of 1910 by Doctor Macnab. In this drawing, beside the materialised figure of a young girl, stands M. Eliphas de Saint-Elme de Taillebourg de la Nox and his light.

Theophrastus gazed silently upon the radiant visage of M. Eliphas de la Nox (it would be unfair on the ink of the printer to give him his full name every time I mention him). Then, since he felt a sudden strong sympathy with this radiant being into whose presence he had been so suddenly introduced, in spite of having found him in a frame he thought almost diabolic, he plucked up courage and resolved to learn the meaning of all the strange things he had seen.

"I don't know where I am," he said somewhat plaintively. "But since I see my friend Adolphe and my wife Marceline with you, I feel reassured. I should like very much to know your name."

"My friend, I am called Eliphas de Saint-Elme de Taillebourg de la Nox."

"You're really called all that?" said Theophrastus, who was beginning to recover his spirits.

The radiant being bowed his head gravely.

"Well, after all, there's nothing very astonishing in that," said Theophrastus. "My name, my real name, my actual family name, is Cartouche; and for a long time everybody has believed that it was a nickname."

"Your name is *not* Cartouche; it is Theophrastus Longuet," said M. Eliphas de la Nox with gentle firmness.

"The one does not prevent the other," said Theophrastus, who better than anyone else knew what he was talking about, quite logically.

"I beg your pardon," said M. Eliphas de la Nox, with the same gentle firmness. "You must not cherish this confusion of mind. *Once upon a time* your name was Cartouche, but *now* it is Theophrastus Longuet. Understand that: *you are* Theophrastus Longuet. My friend, listen to me carefully, as you would listen to a physician who was going to heal you. For you are ill, my friend, very ill, exactly because you believe you are Cartouche, when you are really Theophrastus Longuet. I appeal to all the simplicity of your soul."

"That's all right," said Theophrastus. "I like simple things myself; so I dislike very much, very much indeed, the way by which one comes to see you, through a labyrinth of passages, with skeletons hanging up in them. What's he doing in your house, by the way, that skeleton, instead of resting quietly on Saint-Chaumont Hill? *I recognised him at once.* They were dragging him to the charnel-house at the Gallows of Montfaucon the very day of my marriage with my dear wife Marie-Antoinette Neron, when we were having our wedding breakfast at the Chopinettes. Beaulieu and Old Easy-Going were with us. At that epoch, my dear M. Eliphas de Taillepot—"

"Eliphas de Taillebourg," corrected Adolphe in a somewhat shocked tone.

"At that epoch—my friend Adolphe, who's as serious as a donkey, will tell you so—they no longer hung people at the Gallows of Montfaucon, but they used to throw into the charnel-house of those gallows the remains of people whom they hung elsewhere. That's how it was that this poor Gastelard, whose skeleton I recognised just now, was dragged to the charnel-house after having been hung in the Place de Grève. Gastelard, my dear M. St. Elmo's-Fire—"

"De Saint-Elme," M. Lecamus corrected him again.

"My dear M. de Saint-Elme, Gastelard wasn't up to much, a poor beggar full of imagination, who, having one day disguised himself as a King's deputy, demanded his sword from a gentleman, showing him at the same time an Order of Committal. The gentleman believed that he was being duly arrested, and handed over his sword, the hilt of which was gold and the most beautiful you ever saw. The story ended with Gastelard at the end of a rope. But I'll be hanged, my dear M. de l'Equinox—"

"De la Nox," insisted Adolphe.

"De la Nose, my dear M. de la Nose, I'll be hanged if I ever expected that I should one day find his skeleton in a house in Huchette Street!"

The Mage, motionless and silent, regarded Theophrastus and his talk with an attention nothing could divert.

"I have never laughed anywhere so much as at Saint-Chaumont Hill, between Chopinettes mill and Cock mill," said Theophrastus with the same garrulous cheerfulness. "Chopinettes tavern was there; it had taken the place of the tavern François Villon was so fond of, where for centuries all the cullies and doxies of Paris used to come on hanging-days to carouse. It was between Chopinettes mill, Cock mill and the Gallows of Montfaucon that I buried my treasures; and if you have a plan of old Paris, my dear M. Elephant de Taillepot de St. Elmo's Fire de la Nose—"

Theophrastus had not quite come to the end of his host's name, when, of a sudden, the darkness fled; and the room and all in it shone clear in the brilliant light of day.

He looked round him with manifest satisfaction, at his wife, who was muttering a prayer, at his friend Adolphe, who was on the verge of tears, at the bookshelves, which practically walled the room, and at M. Eliphas de la Nox, who smiled at him with gentle compassion. The Mage had lost his supernatural air; his cloak of astral light had gone; and if his features had still their sublime and ineffable pallor, he none the less looked a man like anybody else.

"I like this a good deal better," said Theophrastus with a deep sigh of relief.

The Mage raised his hand. "No: I will not give you a map of old Paris to look at, though I have them of every age," he said. "You have nothing to do with old Paris. You are Theophrastus Longuet; and we are in the year 1911."

"That's all very well. But it's a question of my treasure, treasures which belong to me," said Theophrastus stubbornly. "And I have every right to look in a map of old Paris at the place where I formerly buried my treasures, in order that I may see on a map of new Paris where I shall have to hunt again. It's clear—"

The Mage interrupted him, saying to M. Lecamus, "I have often seen here crises of Karma; but it has never been my privilege to study one of such force."

"Oh, but so far you've seen nothing—nothing at all!" cried Theophrastus.

The Mage reflected a moment; then he took Theophrastus to a map of the Paris of to-day which hung on the wall of this great library, and pointed out to him the exact spot on which had stood Chopinettes mill, Cock mill, and the Gallows of Montfaucon. Then he laid his finger in the middle of the triangle they formed, and said: "Here is where you must hunt, my friend, to recover your treasures. But all this quarter has been altered again and again; and I very much doubt whether your treasures will still be found where you buried them. I have shown you the spot on a modern map, to clear your mind of the matter. For, my friend, *you must clear your mind*. You must not dwell on your treasures. You must not live in the past. *It is a crime.* You must live in the present, that is to say, *for the Future*. My friend, you must drive out Cartouche, because Cartouche is no more. It is Theophrastus Longuet *who is*."

The Mage pronounced these words in a tone of the most solemn earnestness. Theophrastus smiled at him sadly, and said: "I'm very much obliged to you for your interest in me; and I will not hide from you the fact that I find you extremely sympathetic, in spite of your skeletons and the odd words which crawl about your walls. You must be very learned indeed, to judge from all these shelves full of books. And you must be very good-hearted, for you have certainly treated me with the greatest kindness; but I tell you—and sorry I am to say it—that you can do nothing for me. For unfortunately, my dear sir, you think that I'm ill; but I'm not ill at all. If I were ill, I've no doubt that you'd cure me, but one doesn't cure a man who's not ill. You say to me, you must drive out Cartouche. It's a grand thing to say, splendid; but I don't believe it, my dear M. Elephant de Brandebourg de St. Elmo's Fire de la Box."

But the Mage took his hand, and said with unchanged kindliness:

"None the less Cartouche must be *driven out, for if we do not succeed in driving him out*, we shall have to *kill him*; and I will not conceal from you, my dear M. Longuet, the fact that that is an exceedingly difficult operation."

"When the Man of Light," says Theophrastus in his memoirs, "undertook to relieve me of this obsession by Cartouche, which was not, alas! a matter of imagination but a very real thing, I could only smile pitifully at his vast conceit. But when I understood that he proposed to drive him out by the sole miracle of the reason, I thought it was time to serve the Mage up hot at Charenton lunatic asylum.

"But presently, when he had explained the matter more fully to me, and I began to understand his theory and method, I found myself in full agreement with him and ready to serve his purpose of driving Cartouche out of me by the sole miracle of the reason. Indeed I came in the end to appreciate the vast abyss which separated the Man of Light from my friend Adolphe, the vast abyss which will always separate the Man of Reason from the Learned Ape.

"First of all, he assured me that I had been Cartouche. He was assured of it. And furthermore it was the most natural thing in the world. He said he had scolded Adolphe for having presented my case to him as exceptional, when my case was the case of everybody. Of course, everybody has not been Cartouche. But everybody has been, before their existence of to-day, a good many other people, among whom may very well have been found persons every whit as bad as Cartouche.

"You understand the Man of Light: mine was an every-day case. Everybody has lived before living and will live again. He told me that it was 'The Law of Karma.' *One is being born all the time; one never dies. And when one dies, it is that one is being born again, and so on from the beginning of beginnings!*

"It is understood that at each birth the personality differs from the preceding and succeeding personalities, but each is only a modification of the divine and spiritual ego. These different personalities are in a way only the rings in the infinite chain of life which constitutes throughout the ages our Immortal Individuality.

"And then the Man of Light told me that when one has grasped this immense truth, one should not be astonished that some of the events of *to-day* recall some of the events of *long-ago*. But in order to live according to the law of wisdom one should live in the present and never look backward. I had looked backward too much. My spirit, badly guided by M. Lecamus, had during the last few weeks been wholly occupied with the *long-ago*; and undoubtedly, if that had gone on, I should soon have been reduced to a state dangerously near to that of madness. I ought to be no more astonished at having had another state of soul two hundred years ago than I ought to be astonished at having had another state of soul twenty years ago. Was it that the Theophrastus of to-day had any connection with the Theophrastus of twenty years ago? Certainly not. The Theophrastus of to-day ignored that young man; he even disapproved of him. Would it not be stupid indeed to devote all my faculties to reviving the Theophrastus of twenty years ago? Therefore the great mistake I had made had been only to live for Cartouche, because I had chanced to remember that I had once been Cartouche.

"I tell you that I found the words of M. Elephant de la Box indeed refreshing. They did me a world of good.

"He also told me other things which I shall remember if I live to be a thousand years old. He told me that what are called 'Vocations' in the men of to-day are only latent revelations of their past lives; that what is called 'Facility' is only a retrospective sympathy for objects with which they are better acquainted than with anything else, because they made a more careful study of them before this actual life; and that is the only explanation of it.

"Thereupon he pressed me to his bosom, as a father embraces his child; he breathed upon my eyes and brow his healing breath; and he asked me if I was now persuaded of this truth, and realised that to live happily it was necessary to bear in mind our condition of perpetual change, and that by doing so we should learn to live in the Present and to understand that the whole of time belonged to us.

"I wept with joy, and my dear wife wept with joy, and Adolphe wept with joy. I assured the Man of Light that I understood and believed, that I was no longer astonished that I had been Cartouche, though I was somewhat distressed by the fact, but that it was, after all, so natural that I should never again give it a moment's thought. I cried:

"'Be at ease! Let us all be at ease! Let us live in *the Present*! *Cartouche is driven out!*'

"Thereupon Marceline asked what time it was; and Adolphe answered that it was eleven o'clock. I pulled out my onion and saw that it was half-past eleven. Then, since my watch keeps perfect time, I declared that it was half-past eleven.

"'No. I beg your pardon, but it's eleven o'clock,' said Adolphe.

"'You can cut off my finger if it isn't half-past eleven!" I cried; for I was sure of my watch.

"But the Man of Light looked at his watch and assured me that it was only eleven o'clock. My friend Adolphe was right; and I was sorry for it—on account of my finger. I am an honourable man and an honest manufacturer. I have always kept my word; and no bill of mine has ever been dishonoured. I did not hesitate. Could I have done otherwise?

"'Very well,' I said to Adolphe. 'I owe you a finger.'

"And seizing a small stone tomahawk, which lay on the desk of the Man of Light and was evidently used as a paper-weight, I raised it in the air, and was bringing it down on the little finger of my left hand which I had stuck well out on the corner of the desk—I had the right to give Adolphe the little finger of my left hand; for I had only said to him, 'You can cut off my finger,' without stipulating which finger; and I chose the finger the loss of which would inconvenience me the least. My little finger then would infallibly have been cut off, had not the Man of Light caught my wrist in a grip of steel and held it firmly.

"He bade me put down the tomahawk. I answered that I would not put down the tomahawk till I had cut off my finger which belonged to Adolphe.

"Adolphe exclaimed that my finger was of no use to him, and I could keep it. Marceline joined her entreaties to his, and begged me to keep my finger, since Adolphe made me a present of it. But I answered him that there was no reason for him to make me presents at this season of the year; and I answered her that she knew nothing at all about business.

"Then M. Eliphraste de l'Equinox pointed out that I was not observing the conditions of the contract: I had said, 'You can cut off my finger'; consequently it was the privilege of Adolphe to cut off my finger.

"I admired this exact logic, which indeed never failed him; and I put down my tomahawk.

"I was wrong to put down my tomahawk in that house in Huchette Street; for they flung themselves upon me, and the Man of Light cried:

"'*Come on! It's too late! The only thing to do is to kill him!*'"

XIV

The Operation Begins

It is to M. Lecamus that we owe the account of the operation which M. Eliphas de Saint-Elme de Taillebourg de la Nox thought it his duty to perform on Theophrastus Longuet. His account of it, apparently written for the Pneumatic Club, at the instance of Theophrastus himself, is among the papers in the sandalwood box. It runs:

"The scene of savagery which would have ended in my poor friend Theophrastus losing the little finger of his left hand, but for the presence of mind of M. Eliphas de la Nox, proved to us that the bloodthirsty imagination of Cartouche had absolutely filled the brain of that honest man, my best and trustiest friend. It seemed to us therefore that the sole cure for this terrible evil was *the death of Cartouche*.

"M. de la Nox, indeed, did not hesitate; he had tried reason in vain, though for a moment we had believed it victorious: an operation was indicated. Madame Longuet made a few protests, so half-hearted that we ignored them. As for Theophrastus, it was useless to ask his opinion. Besides, M. de la Nox had already fixed him with his gaze; and no one has ever resisted the gaze of M. de la Nox.

"Theophrastus breathed several deep sighs, and began to tremble violently. But when M. de la Nox cried: 'I order you to sleep, Cartouche!' he fell back into the armchair behind him and never stirred. His breathing was so faint that we might almost have doubted that he was still living.

"The operation of the death of Cartouche was about to begin. I knew, from several famous instances, that it was an operation of great difficulty, for one always risks, in essaying to kill a reincarnate soul, that is to say, to cast back into nothingness that part of the Individuality which has been someone in a previous existence, and pursues us into this with a violence which prevents us from living in the Present—one always risks, I say, *killing along with the reincarnate soul the body in which it is reincarnate*. We were going to try to kill Cartouche without killing Theophrastus, *but we might kill Theophrastus*. Hence our anxiety.

"It needed all the authority, all the science, and also the absolute calmness of M. de la Nox to render me at all at ease in the extremity in which we found ourselves. But M. de la Nox has the most powerful and dominating will the world has known since Jacques Molay, whom he has succeeded in the supreme command of the actual and secret Order of the Templars.

"Also I bore in mind the categorical demonstrations of his last treatise on Psychical Surgery, and the exact precision of his instructions in his monograph on the *Astral Scalpel*. My trust in M. de la Nox, and the criminal eccentricity of poor Theophrastus, of which the ears of the wretched Signor Petito had been the first victims and filled me with dread of irremediable catastrophes, led me to consider the operation of the death of Cartouche, in spite of its danger, the best course in these painful circumstances.

"We carried the sleeping Theophrastus down into the basement, into the psychical laboratory of the Mage, which is lighted night and day by great hissing flames of a crimson gas of the nature of which I am ignorant.

"We laid Theophrastus down on a camp-bed; and for more than a quarter of an hour M. de la Nox gazed at him in a marvellous stillness. We were silent. At last an admirable melody was heard. It was the voice of M. de la Nox praying. Of what angelic music, of what empyrean vibrations, of what syllables of heavenly glory and triumphant love, was that prayer composed! Who shall ever repeat it? Who shall ever re-compose it? Do you know the musician, incomparable Master of sound, who shall re-compose, once they have passed, the elements of that fragrant breeze of Spring which chants, for the first time, under the first leaves, its trembling song of hope and eternal life, on the threshold of the recurring seasons?

"I only know that that prayer began somewhat like this:

'In the beginning, you were Silence, Æon eternal, source of Æons! Silent, as thou wert, was Eunoia, and ye contemplated one another in an inexpressible embrace, Æon, source of Æons, Eunoia, source of love, fruitful germ from which the Abyss should bring forth life! In the beginning, you were the Silence, source of Æons!' . . .

"When the prayer came to an end, M. de la Nox took the hand of Theophrastus and commanded him. But since the lips of M. de la Nox did not move, since he commanded without speaking, and questioned Theophrastus through the sole interpreter of his dominating will, I only learnt what his commands and questions had been from the answers of the sleeping Theophrastus.

"Theophrastus began without any apparent effort or suffering:

"'Yes; I see. . . Yes; I am. . .

"'. . . . .

"'I'm Theophrastus Longuet. . .

"'. . . . .

"'In a flat in Gerando Street. . .'

"M. de la Nox turned towards us, and said in a low voice: 'The operation is not going well. I put Cartouche to sleep; and it is Theophrastus who is answering. He is asleep in the Present. It would be dangerous to be abrupt. I am going to let him move about in *the Present* for a while.'

"Theophrastus began to speak again:

"'I'm in Gerando Street, in the flat above my own. I see stretched on a bed an earless man. Facing him is a woman—a dark woman—young and pretty—her name is Regina—'

"'. . . . .

"'The pretty young woman. . . whose name is Regina. . . is speaking to the earless man. . . She is saying:

"'"As sure as my name's Regina, you'll see no more of me, and you'll never hear the 'Carnival of Venice' again, if in forty-eight hours from now you haven't found some way of making a big enough income to support me properly. When I married you, Signor Petito, you deceived me shamefully about the amount of your fortune and the character of your intelligence. A nice thing that fortune of yours, Signor Petito! We're two quarters behind with the rent; and unless we wish to lose our furniture, we must shoot the moon. And as for your intelligence! Well, when a woman is young and pretty like I am, she wants a husband with enough intelligence to find the money to pay her dressmaker's bill. Am I to go back to my mother, or are you going to do it?"

"'The earless man is speaking. . . He says:

"'"Oh, shut up, Regina, you're only making my head ache. Can't you leave me in peace to discover the hiding-place of the treasures, which the silly fool downstairs is incapable of getting out of the earth?"

"'The silly fool,' said the sleeping Theophrastus, 'is Cartouche!'

"'I was waiting for that word,' said M. de la Nox quickly. 'Now I can make him quit *the Present*! Pray, madame! pray, my friend! the hour has come! *I am going to tempt Providence!*'

"Then, raising his hand above the brow of my sleeping friend, he said in a voice of command impossible, utterly impossible, to disobey:

'Cartouche, what were you doing at ten o'clock at night on the First of April, 1721?'

"'At ten o'clock at night on the First of April, 1721,' said the sleeping Theophrastus without a moment's hesitation, 'I tap sharply twice on the door of the Queen Margot tavern. . . After the row I should never have believed that I could have got so easily to Ferronnerie Street. . . But I did for the horse of the French Guard, or rather he fell down near the pump at Notre-Dame. . . I have thrown my pursuers off my track. . . At the Queen Margot I find Patapon, Saint James's Gate, and Black-mug. . . Pretty-Milkmaid is with them. . . I tell them the story over a bottle of ratafia. . . I trusted them; and I tell them that I suspect Old Easy-Going, and perhaps Marie-Antoinette herself, of having whispered something to the Police. . . They all protested. . . But I shout louder than they; and they are quiet. . . I tell them that I have made up my mind to deal faithfully with all those who give me any reason to suspect them. I get into a fine rage. . . Pretty-Milkmaid says that there's no longer any living with me. . . It's true that there's no longer any living with me. . . But is it my fault? . . . Everybody betrays me. I can't sleep two nights running in the same place. . . Where are the days when I had all Paris on my side? The day of my wedding with Marie-Antoinette? The day when at the Little Seal tavern in Faubourg-Saint-Antoine Street, we sang in chorus:

"Guzzle, cullies, and booze away,
Till Gabriel's trump on Judgment Day!"

We ate partridge that day—that was more than the King did—we drank champagne. My beautiful Marie-Antoinette loved me dearly. My Uncle and Aunt Tanton were there. And all that happiness was only last May, the fifteenth of last May! . . . And now! . . . Where is Uncle Tanton now? Shut up in the Châtelet. . . And his son? . . . I had to kill him last month to prevent him denouncing me! . . . I was quick about it. . . One pistol bullet at Montparnasse, and the body in a ditch; and I was sure of his silence. . . But how many more to kill? . . . How many more to kill to be sure of the silence of all? . . . By the throttle of Madame Phalaris! I had to kill Pepin, the Archer, and Huron the King's Deputy who were in full cry after me one evening, and five archers besides whom I massacred, poor beggars! in Mazarine Street. . . *I see their five corpses still*. . . And yet I'm not at all bad-natured! . . . I don't want to hurt anybody. . . I only ask one thing, to be allowed to quietly police Paris, for everybody's security. . . My chief councillor himself is grumbling. He doesn't forgive my executing Jacques Lefebvre. . . Of course, there's no living with me any longer; but it's only because I wish to live!

"'After that little talk I leave them. . . I look out of the door of the Queen Margot: Ferronnerie Street is empty. I hurry off; and near the Cemetery of the Innocents I meet Madeline. . . But I don't tell her where I am going. . . As a matter of fact, I am going to spend the night in my hole in Amelot Street like a wretched thief! . . . It's pouring with rain.'"

M. Adolphe Lecamus declares that he has given us the exact words which came from the lips of Theophrastus in his hypnotic sleep, but that he has not been able to give us the modulation of these phrases, their strange tones, their sudden stops, their hurried starts, and their often dolorous endings. He makes no attempt to describe the physiognomy of Theophrastus. At times it expressed anger, at times scorn, sometimes extravagant daring, sometimes terror. Sometimes, he declares, at certain moving moments, *Theophrastus was exactly like the portrait of Cartouche*.

M. de la Nox was desirous of bringing Cartouche to the hour of his death by slow degrees. He feared the shock of making him abruptly live it over again. Therefore he had taken him back to the First of April, 1721.

The minutes which followed were exceedingly painful for us, as the wretched Cartouche once more went through the agony of those last months amid the perpetual treachery of his lieutenants and the incredible, dogged animosity of the police.

The narrative of M. Lecamus, painful as it is, presents no new fact. It merely corroborates history. There is, indeed, nothing to be gained by descending to the laboratory of M. Eliphas de la Nox to acquire a knowledge of the sensational arrest and imprisonment in the Grand-Châtelet. We find in the Register of the Orders of Committal of the King:

"May 16, 1721, Order of the King to seize and arrest one Cartouche, who has murdered Sire Huron, Lieutenant of the Short Robe, and one Tanton; and also Cartouche Cadet, called Louison; the Chevalier, called Cracksman; and Fortier, called Mouchy, for complicity in the murders."

On the margin against the name of Cartouche is written the single word, "*Broken.*"

That arrest was much easier to order than to effect. It was not till October 14, 1721, that treachery bore its fruit, and we can read the report of Jean de Coustade, paymaster of the company of Chabannes, forty-seven years old, twenty-seven years' service.

M. de Coustade took with him forty men and four sergeants, of whose trustworthiness he was assured by Duchâtelet (Lieutenant of Cartouche, who was betraying him, himself a sergeant of the French Guards; they had promised him a pardon), dressed as civilians, with their weapons hidden, and surrounded the house in which Duchâtelet had informed him that Cartouche was lying. It was a little after nine at night that they arrived at the Pistol Inn, kept by Germain Savard and his wife, at Courtille, near High Borne (Trois-Bornes Street).

Savard was smoking his pipe on his door-step; and Duchâtelet said to him, "Is there anyone upstairs?"

"No," said Savard.

"Are the four ladies here?"

"Up you go!" said Savard, who was waiting for these words.

He stepped aside; and the whole troop dashed upstairs to attack Cartouche.

"When we entered the chamber upstairs," writes M. Jean de Coustade in his report, "we found Balagny and Limousin drinking wine in front of the fire. Gaillard was in bed, and Cartouche sitting on the side of the bed, mending his breeches. We threw ourselves on him. The stroke was so unexpected that he had no time to make any resistance. We bound him with thick ropes, took him first to the house of the Secretary of State for War, and then, on foot, to the Grand-Châtelet, as soon as the order was given."

As a matter of fact the affair was by no means as simple as M. de Coustade relates, though it ended as he says. In spite of his short stature, Cartouche was of exceptional strength; and they only overcame him and bound him to a pillar after a furious struggle.

At last, after all precautions had been taken, they put him in a coach. He was in his shirt only; for he had not had time to put on the breeches he was mending. Since they hustled him fiercely, he said: "Look out, lads, you're ruffling my clothes!"

He had retained all his usual calm; and he congratulated the lieutenant who had betrayed him on the fine clothes he was wearing that day. In truth, Duchâtelet had come out dressed in a very fine new black suit, on account of the death of the Duchess Marguerite d'Orleans, who had died a fortnight before. On the way, as the coach just missed crushing an unfortunate wayfarer, Cartouche once more uttered the words of which he was so fond: "*We must avoid the wheel!*"

From the house of the Secretary of State for War he went on foot in the middle of a grand escort. Half the people of Paris rushed out of their houses to see him pass, crying, "It's Cartouche!" without any strong belief that it was. They had been deceived so many times. But they perceived that it was true, when an officer of the escort struck the prisoner with his cane, and the prisoner turned quietly round and gave him a kick on the jaw with his left foot, which sent him head over heels into the gutter. The crowd applauded, for it has a great affection for robbers—when they are taken.

In the Grand-Châtelet Prison Cartouche was visited by all the Polite World. The Regent went out of his way to express his personal regret at this sad event. "But," said he, "my sovereign duties impose this unpleasant duty on me." The ladies of the Court vied with one another in their attentions to the prisoner. They refused him nothing. He had three pints of wine a day.

He had never been so much the fashion. At once a play was produced entitled "Cartouche." Legrand, its author, and Quinault, who took the principal part, came to ask him for information about details of the production. At last, when Cartouche had sufficiently amused himself, he turned his attention to escape. In spite of the unceasing watch they kept on him, he was on the very point of success, having got out of his cell and by means of a rope twisted from the straw of his mattress, made his way down into a shop, when they caught him as he was drawing the last bolt of a door which separated him from the street. They found that the Grand-Châtelet was not safe enough for a man of such ingenuity; and he was secretly carried in chains to the Conciergerie, and imprisoned in the most secure corner of Montgomery Tower.

XV

The Operation Ends

Firm in his intention of bringing his subject to his death by slow degrees, M. Eliphas de la Nox took Theophrastus slowly through the imprisonment, trial, and condemnation of Cartouche. But I omit that part of the narrative of M. Lecamus, since the historians have described that imprisonment and trial at length. I take it up at the point at which Cartouche was on his way to the Torture-chamber that they might force from him the names of his accomplices.

"And now," says M. Lecamus in his narrative, "we were approaching the crucial point of the operation: *to kill Cartouche without killing Theophrastus*. Simple enough words, but the most difficult operation in Psychic Surgery. Truly M. de la Nox had been right when he said that he was about to tempt Providence. Truly, he had assumed the most appalling responsibility, the risk of killing Theophrastus without killing Cartouche, and consequently of letting that fiend in human form again become reincarnate in some unfortunate contemporary.

"But then it was M. Eliphas de Saint-Elme de Taillebourg de la Nox who had assumed the responsibility, the greatest living expert in Psychical Surgery, the delicacy of whose Astral Scalpel is known to the initiates throughout the world, even to far Thibet. He knew how to move the spirit, quietly and calmly, *round its own death*, so preparing it for the last moment. *He made his dead man live till the very moment at which he made his dead man die!*

"He had brought Theophrastus-Cartouche to the hour when his jailors took him from his cell to lead him to the Torture-chamber. His next question was:

"'And where are you now, Cartouche?'

"'I am going down a little staircase at the end of Straw Alley. . . They are opening a grating. . . I am in the darkness of the cellars. . . These cellars frighten me. . . I know them well. . . Ah, yes: I was shut up in these cellars in the days of Philippe-le-Bel!'

"M. de la Nox raised his voice in a tone of awful command, and said:

"'Cartouche! You *are* Cartouche! You are in those cellars by order of the *Regent*!'

"Then he muttered, 'Philippe-le-Bel! Where in Heaven's name are we going now? We must not stray. We must not! Where are you now, Cartouche?'

"'I am going deeper into the night of the cellars, I am surrounded by guards—many guards. It is too dark to see how many. . . Ah! I see at the end there, right at the end, a ray which I know well. *It is a square ray which the sun has forgotten there since the beginning of the history of France!* . . . My guards are not French Guards, they distrust all the French Guards. My guards are commanded by the military lieutenant of the Châtelet.'

"There was a pause as M. de la Nox let Cartouche continue on his painful way; then he said: 'And where are you now, Cartouche?'

"'I am in the Torture-chamber. . . About me are men dressed in long robes. . . Their faces are masked. . . They are binding me to the stool of Question. . . They are thick ropes. . . Well, they need them thick for me. . . But if they think they're going to get anything out of me, they're wrong—altogether wrong!'

"The face of Theophrastus was set in an expression of stubborn pride, almost ferocious. Slowly it weakened in intensity as we stood waiting and watching him; then suddenly it changed to an expression of pain, and he uttered an ear-splitting yell.

"M. de la Nox and I started back; Marceline uttered a cry.

"Plainly M. de la Nox did not expect that yell, for he said in a tone of surprise, 'Why did you yell like that, Cartouche?'

"'I yell because it's so awful *not to be able to denounce my accomplices*! Their names are on the tip of my tongue; but they won't come off it! Can't they see that if I don't denounce them, it's because I can't move the tip of my tongue? Why didn't Cartouche move the tip of his tongue? I can't; and it's most unfair!'

"M. de la Nox was silent for a while. There was no reason why he should harrow our sensibilities with the pangs of that old-world ruffian. It was bad enough to see the anguished face of Theophrastus. After a while it grew serene again; and M. de la Nox said:

"'And what are you doing now, Cartouche?'

"'They are leaving me alone,' said Theophrastus. 'Only the doctor and the surgeon are feeling my pulse. . . They are congratulating themselves on having chosen the torture of the Boot, because it is least dangerous to life, and the least liable to accidents.'

"I observed that he spoke in his ordinary voice, that it was not weakened by the pain he had suffered. It seemed as if he only felt it at the moment of its actual infliction, that he did not feel the after pain.

"There came another long pause; then suddenly Theophrastus uttered another ear-splitting yell.

"'What's the matter now, Cartouche?' said M. de la Nox anxiously.

"'It's the tip of my tongue!' cried Theophrastus furiously.' Can't these silly fools see that the names are on the tip of my tongue, and won't come off it? Why don't the idiots take them off it? Is it my fault that Cartouche didn't split?'

"'But Cartouche was silent: why are you yelling?' said M. de la Nox.

"'*They're torturing Cartouche; but it's Theophrastus Longuet who yells!*'

"M. de la Nox seemed thunderstruck by this response. He turned and said to us in a trembling voice: 'Then—then it's *he* who suffers.'

"It was the truth; one could not doubt it to see the anguish on the contorted face of Theophrastus. It was Cartouche who was tortured and Theophrastus who suffered. That proved the *identity* of the soul; *but it also proved that the pain had not ceased to be effective after two hundred years*. That was what dismayed M. de la Nox. It was the first time that a case of this kind had come under his observation during his operations with the Astral Scalpel. The pain of Cartouche found voice through two centuries; this cry of anguish which had not issued from his stubborn lips, *had waited two hundred years to burst from the lungs of Theophrastus Longuet*!

"M. Eliphas de la Nox buried his head, his luminous head, in his hands and prayed ardently: 'In the beginning you were the Silence! Æon eternal! Source of Æons! . . .'

"At the end of the prayer he felt Theophrastus' pulse and listened carefully to the beating of his heart. Then he said:

"'M. Longuet is plainly a man of strong constitution, and thoroughly sound. In fact, from that point of view there's scarcely anything to fear. *He will bury Cartouche.* I think we ought to go through with the operation.'

"I said that I was of his opinion. Marceline hesitated a little, and then bade him continue.

"'And now what are they doing, Cartouche?' said M. de la Nox.

"'They keep asking me those useless questions; but I can't answer,' said Theophrastus impatiently. 'And I keep asking myself what that man in the right-hand corner of the cell is doing. He has his back turned to me; and I can hear a *sound of clinking iron*. . . The executioner is at the moment taking it easily. He's leaning against the wall and yawning. . . There's a lamp on the table which lights up two men who keep on writing and writing. What they're writing I can't conceive, for I haven't said anything—I can't. It's the man in the corner that puzzles me. There's a red light on the wall as if he were between me and a brazier. I wonder what those irons are he's messing about with.'

"'It must be the red-hot irons. They used them,' said M. de la Nox; and he shivered.

"We were silent; and presently there came a series of dreadful, ear-splitting yells from Theophrastus. M. de la Nox turned a very pale and troubled face to us, and declared that he had never come across, or even suspected that one could come across, pain so *effective*. He had no doubt that it must be owing to the fact that he had never before operated on souls reincarnate after an interval of less than five hundred years; that even those were very rare; and the bulk of his clientele was composed of souls at least two thousand years old. I fancied that he was somewhat out of his depth; and it surprised me beyond words.

"Again Theophrastus yelled; then suddenly Marceline cried:

"'Look! Look, his hair!'

"The most surprising sight met our eyes: *the hair of Theophrastus was turning white*!

"The whiteness spread over it as smoothly as the edge of the rising tide spreads over the sand, but more slowly. In five minutes all his hair had turned white except one lock on his brow.

"We were silent; and I wiped the perspiration from my face. M. de la Nox was panting; Marceline was sobbing. Somehow that slow whitening of the hair was more painful, more impressively dreadful than those piercing, ear-splitting yells.

"M. de la Nox seemed almost at his wits' end. Twice I saw him open his lips to question Theophrastus; twice he shut them without a word. Then suddenly he stooped down and listened to the beating of Theophrastus' heart. He stood upright again with an air of relief and said:

"'What are you doing now, Cartouche?'

"'Shamming dead. After the red-hot irons and the boiling water they poured into my ears I shammed dead. They have left me. . . I am slipping the paper I wrote in my cell this morning, with a splinter of wood, and my blood, into the crack in the wall above my head. It tells where I've hid my treasures.'

"He was silent again; and again I saw the face of M. de la Nox grow intent as once more he concentrated all his being on his astral work. How I wished I had attained a height of psychic development which would have enabled me to follow the wonderful, the miraculous movements of his Astral Scalpel.

"It must have been nearly three-quarters of an hour later that he heaved a deep sigh and said, 'Our work is nearly at an end. Where are you now, Cartouche?'

"'I don't know quite what has happened,' said Theophrastus. 'I hid the document; and I have not seen anyone since. When I open my eyes—it is rather an effort—I do not recognise the place to which they have brought me. . . I'm certainly not in the Torture-chamber, nor in my cell in Montgomery Tower. . . There's a faint blue light falling through the bars of a grating in front of me. . . The moon is coming to visit me. . . The moonlight has descended two or three of the steps which lead up from the grating. . . I try to move. . . I can't. . . I'm a log. My will no longer commands my muscles or limbs. . . It's as if all relations between my will and my body had ceased. . . My brain is only master of my sight and understanding. It is no longer master of my actions. . . My poor limbs! I feel them *scattered* round about me. . . I must have reached the point of suffering at which one suffers no more. . . But where am I? . . . The moonlight descends two more steps. . . And again two more steps. . . Ah! what is that it lights up? . . . An eye—a big eye. . . The moonlight moves. . . A skull. . . The moonlight moves. . . A bony hand! . . . I understand! I understand! They have thrown me into a common grave! . . . The moonlight moves. . . There are two legs of a dead man lying across my body! . . . I recognise those steps now! . . . And that grating! . . . I am in the charnel-house of Montfaucon! . . . *I am frightened!*

"'When I used to go up the street of the Dead to carouse at the Chopinettes, I often looked through that grating. I looked through it curiously because I saw that one day I should lie in the charnel-house. But never did it occur to me that when a body lay there, *it could look out from the other side of the grating*! And now my body looks out through it! They have thrown me into the charnel-house because they believed me dead! I am buried alive with the bodies of hanged men! My wretched fate surpasses anything that the imagination of men could invent!

"'The saddest reflections assail me. I ask myself by what trick of Fate I am reduced to such an extremity. I am forced to confess that Fate played no part in the matter. It was my pride, nothing but my accursed pride. I could have quietly remained King of all the robbers, *if there had been any living with me*. Pretty-Milkmaid was right when she said at the Queen Margot *that there was no longer any living with me*. I would no longer listen to a word from anyone; and when I called together my Grand Council, I took no notice whatever of the resolutions it passed. I took a delight in playing the despot; and I ended with that mania for cutting up everyone I suspected into little bits. My lieutenants ran greater risks in serving me than in disobeying me. They betrayed me; and it was quite logical. *Oh, it's quite time for these reflections, now that I'm in the charnel-house!*

"'I'm alive in this charnel-house, alive among the dead; and for the first time in my life *I am frightened*.'

"Theophrastus was silent for a minute; and we looked at one another with harried eyes. Then in the same mournful, plaintive tones he took up his tale again.

"'It's odd—very odd. Now that I'm on the very boundary of life and death my senses perceive things which they could not perceive when I was in health. My ears hear no more—that boiling water destroyed my hearing—*yet they do hear*. There is a footfall, a slinking footfall on the steps leading down to the grating. . . Suddenly the moon ceases to light the charnel-house. . . Then I see between me and the moon on the steps of the charnel-house, a man! a living man! . . . Maybe I am saved! I wanted to cry aloud with joy; and perhaps I should have cried aloud, if the horror of what I *feel*, of what I *know*, had not sealed my lips. I *feel*, I *know* that this man has come to rob me of my hand. . . I read it, clearly, *in his brain*. A lady of the Court has sent him for the charm—the charm to keep her husband's love—the hand of a murderer—the hand of Cartouche!

"'*I read it in his brain as clearly as if I read it written*. . . He is lighting a lantern. . . He has unlocked the grating and entered the charnel-house. . . He has found my body, and is stooping over it. . . He has taken my left hand in his left hand, and his knife gleams in the light of the lantern. . . He is cutting through my wrist. . . I do not feel the blade in my wrist; I see it. . . Ah! I begin to feel the knife! . . . Oh! My wrist! My wrist! . . . It is nearly severed. . . Ah! Ah! Ah! . . . It is severed!

"'What is this. . . The man howls. . . He is dancing about among the dead. . . I see! I see. . . My hand has come away in the left hand of the man who howls, but by a last miracle of the last life in my wrist, *as it was severed*, my hand gripped the hand of the man who howls! . . . Ha! Ha! he can't get rid of it! . . . It's gripped him! . . . How it grips him! . . . He is dragging at it with his right hand! . . . He can't stir it! . . . Ah, it isn't easy to rid oneself of a *dead man's last grip*! . . . He is out of the charnel-house, howling! . . . He bounds up the steps, howling! . . . As he goes, howling, he is waving, like a madman, in the moonlight, *my gripping hand*!'

"The voice of Theophrastus died faintly away; and I heard the teeth of M. de la Nox chatter. Then he whispered:

"'Where are you now, Cartouche?'

"'I am entering the radiant darkness of death!'

XVI

The Drawbacks of Psychic Surgery

As soon as Theophrastus had uttered the words: 'I am entering the radiant darkness of death,' M. Eliphas de Saint-Elme de Taillebourg de la Nox raised his right hand above his head with a splendid gesture, then bent over the face of my friend, breathed upon his eyelids, and said:

"'Theophrastus Longuet, awake!'

"Theophrastus did not awake. His eyelids remained closed, and his stillness appeared to us stiller than ever. And now that he spoke no more, now that his lips were closed as tightly as his eyelids, it suddenly seemed to us, stricken with a horrible dread, that he had followed Cartouche into the radiant darkness of death.

"His corpse-like pallor, his hair grown suddenly white, showed him to us terribly old, old with the age suddenly acquired in the depths of the tomb.

"M. de la Nox breathed on his eyelids again and again; again and again he moved his arms in splendid gestures; again and again he cried:

"'Theophrastus Longuet, awake! Awake! Theophrastus Longuet, awake!'

"Theophrastus did not awake; and our hearts sank and sank; then, at the very moment at which we abandoned hope of his ever awaking, he uttered an appalling groan, opened his eyes, and said quietly:

"'Good-morning. Cartouche is dead,'

"M. de la Nox gasped and said, 'Thank God, the operation has succeeded!'

"Then he began his prayer again: 'In the beginning thou wert the Silence! Æon eternal! Source of Æons! . . .' Marceline and I were shaking the hands of Theophrastus, and laughing hysterically. In all conscience, the operation had been severe; but now that it was successful we congratulated Theophrastus warmly. We congratulated him on having escaped from his terrible plight at the cost of a bottle of hair-dye. It was not much to pay for *the death of Cartouche*.

"Then we bade him get up and come with us. We were in a hurry to get out of the house in Huchette Street. It seemed to us as if we had been in it a good deal more than two hundred years.

"'Come along, dear! Come along!' said Marceline.

"'Speak louder,' said Theophrastus, 'I don't know what's the matter with my ears. I seem to be very deaf; and then I can't move.'

"'You must be a little dazed, dear,' said Marceline. 'And considering the time you've been stretched on this camp-bed without stirring, it isn't to be wondered at. But make an effort and come along.'

"'Speak louder, I tell you!' said Theophrastus impatiently. 'I can move my arms, but I can't move my legs. I want to move them, but they don't stir; and then there's a pricking in my feet.'

"'It's pins and needles, dear. Bend your toes back quickly. I want to get home. We've had nothing to eat since this morning, and I'm dreadfully hungry,' said Marceline.

"'I don't know whether I've got any toes,' said Theophrastus sadly.

"'Come on. It's time we were going,' said I.

"'Undoubtedly; but you'll have to carry me, for my legs are in such a state. . .'

"M. de la Nox uttered a deep groan. He had turned back the socks of Theophrastus and seen his ankles. They were swollen and scarred and bleeding. In half a minute we had slit up the legs of his trousers and pants with a pair of scissors. What a dreadful sight met our eyes! *The legs of Theophrastus were the legs of a man who has suffered the torture of the Boot!*

"M. de la Nox groaned again, and with his eyes full of tears, he said: 'Incredible! incredible! Who could have believed that pain would be so *effective* at the end of two hundred years?'

"'This phenomenon is analogous to the stigmata of the Saints,' I said, suddenly realising its scientifically psychic significance.

"But Marceline burst into tears and flung herself upon the unhappy Theophrastus.

"I shook my fist in the face of Destiny, and hurried out to fetch a cab.

"When I returned, Marceline was still weeping; Theophrastus was still examining his legs with extreme curiosity and inquiring how it was that he could not move them, and how they came to be in this extraordinary condition.

"M. Eliphas de Saint-Elme de Taillebourg de la Nox did not answer; he was kneeling, with his face buried in his hands, sobbing in utter despair.

"He said, or rather sobbed, in a lamentable voice: 'My Beloved! My Beloved! I believed that I was thy son, O My Beloved! I took my shadow for thy light! O My Beloved! Thou hast humbled my pride; I am only a little bit of the Night, at the bottom of the obscure Abyss, I, the Man of Light. And the Night does not *will*! And I have willed, I: the Night! I am only a dark son of the Silence, Æon, Source of Æons! And I have wished to *speak*! Ah, Life! Life! To know Life! To possess Life! To equal Life! . . . Temptation! Vertigo of the eternal Abyss! Mystery of the Ternary! Three! Yes; the three worlds are *one*! And the world is three! It was the truth at Tyre, at Memphis! At Babylon! One! Two! Three! Active, Passive, and Reactive! One and One make two! Two is neuter! But! But! But, O My Beloved! One and Two make Twelve. One is God! Two is matter! Put matter beside God! Pythagoras has said it, and you have Twelve. That means Union! . . . That means? That means? Who then here below has dared to pronounce the words: *That means?*'

"Then he sobbed in the most heart-rending fashion, while Theophrastus on his camp-bed said:

"'I should like very much to get out of this.'"

XVII

Theophrastus Begins to Take an Interest in Things

The unlucky Theophrastus was more than six weeks recovering from his Astral operation. M. Lecamus describes his illness in a somewhat long-winded fashion. Little by little he began to recover the use of his legs; but it seemed unlikely that his hearing would ever quite recover from the boiling water which had deafened Cartouche two hundred years before; at intervals he was for a few moments stone deaf. During all this time he made no allusion to the Past; I do not speak of that wretched past, bounded in the minds of all of us by the few years which have elapsed since our last terrestrial birth; he made no allusion to *his eighteenth-century past*. This fact assured Marceline, M. Lecamus, and M. Eliphas de Saint-Elme de Taillebourg de la Nox, who was a frequent visitor at the sick-bed, that Cartouche was indeed dead; and M. de la Nox was often heard to thank Æon, Source of Æons, for this happy event.

Theophrastus, as his legs healed, had serious thoughts of returning to business. He had retired young, at the age of forty-one, owing to his invention of a superior rubber stamp which had ousted the rubber stamps of rival manufacturers from the market. His mind was full of yet another innovation which would revolutionise the whole Rubber-stamp Industry. There could be no stronger symptom of a complete cure, no stronger proof that the operation had not weakened his mind. And when he began to get about again, Mme. Longuet found that he had become so *natural* that she, and M. Lecamus along with her, believed that their misfortunes had at last tired out Destiny.

Theophrastus would never have his Black Feather again: it had been extirpated for the rest of time.

However, by the instructions of M. Eliphas de Saint-Elme de Taillebourg de la Nox, they kept a careful watch on him. It was his habit to rise at an early hour, and after having breakfasted on a cup of chocolate and buttered toast, go for a stroll on the outer Boulevard. He was trying his legs. He began to find in them their pristine elasticity.

He looked into the shops; he watched with a Parisian's interest the moving panorama of the streets. M. Lecamus, who followed him, observed nothing abnormal in his actions; and in his reports to M. de la Nox he only laid stress on a single fact, truly unimportant, a somewhat prolonged halt before a butcher's stall. If this halt had not been a daily habit, even Adolphe, on the look-out as he was, would have paid no attention to it. Theophrastus, his hands behind his back playing with his green umbrella, would gaze with satisfaction at the red meat. He often had a talk with the butcher, a big, square-shouldered, cheery soul, always ready with some simple joke. One day Adolphe found that Theophrastus was prolonging his halt unduly. He walked up to the stall and found him engaged, with the butcher, in adorning the fresh meat with paper frills. It was a harmless occupation; and so M. de la Nox thought, for there is a note of his on the margin of Adolphe's report: "He can look at the red meat on the butcher's stall. It is just as well to let him 'see red' at times. It is the end of the Psychic crisis, and hurts no one."

Now this butcher, M. Houdry, was famous in his district for the whiteness and delicacy of his veal. His customers often wondered where the calves of M. Houdry were fed. It was a mystery which was making his fortune. In the course of time, Theophrastus won his heart and was admitted to his confidence. The secret of his success lay, not in the fact that his calves were specially fed, but in the fact that he killed them himself and in his method of killing them: he used to slice off their heads with a single stroke of a great cutlass.

As their intimacy increased, Theophrastus was admitted to witness the operation; and he spent many a happy hour in the slaughter-house of the butcher, observing him kill and cut up the calves which were bringing him wealth and fame.

Theophrastus was exceedingly interested in the whole process. He learnt the names of the different instruments with enthusiasm, and was presently allowed to help with the simpler parts of the process. It was a privilege. He came to feel even more than M. Houdry's scorn for the methods of ordinary butchers.

But every day as he left the stall he made the same little joke. He said:

"You kill a calf every day. You must be careful, my dear M. Houdry; or you will find that it will end in the calves getting to know about it."

One day he said, "Look at the calf's eyes, M. Houdry! Look at his eyes!"

"Well, what about them?" said M. Houdry.

"Look how they're looking at you!"

"But they're dead," said M. Houdry, somewhat puzzled.

"And you're not afraid of the eyes of a dead calf which look at you?" said Theophrastus. "I congratulate you on your courage!"

M. Houdry went on with his work, thinking that his pupil had certainly some queer fancies.

When he began to deal with the calf's ears, Theophrastus cried, with angelic delight: "The ears? I understand all about ears! Leave them to me!" And he bought the calf's head.

M. Houdry wished to have it sent to his house, but Theophrastus would not let it out of his hands. He disposed it carefully in the bottom of his green umbrella.

As he went out of the slaughter-house he said: "Au revoir, M. Houdry, I am taking my calf's head away with me; but I have left you the eyes. I should not like the eyes of a calf to look at me as those eyes looked at you just now. The eyes of a dead calf—a nasty thing—very nasty. You laugh, M. Houdry? Well, well, it's your business. . . My congratulations on your courage. But all the same it will end in the calves getting to know about it!"

He returned home; and when he showed Marceline and Adolphe his calf's head in his green umbrella, they smiled at one another.

"He is beginning to take pleasure in things," said Marceline.

"An innocent amusement," said Adolphe indulgently.

XVIII

The Evening Paper

It was the habit of the three friends to play a game of dominoes in the evening after dinner. M. Lecamus, who was a Norman, took a delight in using terms racy of the soil. When he set down the Double-six, he would cry: "Now for the double-nigger!" When he put down a Five, he would cry: "The pup! That bites!" When he put down a One, he would cry: "The maggot! Bait!" The Three drew from him this phrase: "If you've the pluck, down with the pig's-tail!" He called the Two "The beggar!" The unfortunate Four was blasted by the name of "The whelp!" and he could not put down a Blank without announcing: "The washerwoman!"

Marceline took the greatest delight in these exclamations, and she was always ready to play dominoes. Theophrastus generally lost; and it was a pleasure to see him lose, for at this game he had displayed the most disagreeable nature in the world. Whenever he lost, he sulked.

One evening Theophrastus had, as usual, lost; and with an angry frown on his brow, he had stopped playing, and buried himself in an evening paper. He was very fond of the political notes, and his opinions were limited. They were bounded on the north by "The Despotism of Tyrants," and on the south by "The Socialist Utopia." Between the Socialist Utopia and the Despotism of Tyrants, he understood everything, he declared, except that one should attack the army. He often said, "The army must not be touched!" He was a worthy soul.

That evening he read the Political Notes without, as usual, commenting aloud on them, because he was sulking. And then his eyes were caught by this headline:

Cartouche Is Not Dead.

He could not refrain from smiling, so absurd did this hypothesis seem to him. Then he ran his eyes over the first lines of the article, and let escape him the word "Strange! . . ." and then the word "Odd. . ." and then the word "Amazing. . ." But without any particular display of emotion. Then he decided that it was time to stop sulking, and said:

"You haven't read this article entitled: 'Cartouche is not dead,' Adolphe. It's a strange and amazing article."

Marceline and Adolphe started violently and looked at one another in dismay. Theophrastus read:

"Is Cartouche, then, not dead? For some days the police, with the greatest mystery which we however have penetrated, have been solely occupied with a series of strange crimes of which they have been forced to conceal the most curious side from the public. These crimes and *the manner in which their author escapes from the Police at the very moment at which they believe they have caught him*, recall point by point *the methods of the celebrated Cartouche*. If it were not a question of an affair as reprehensible as a series of crimes, one could even admire the art with which the model is imitated. As an official of the Prefecture of Police, whose name we do not give since he insisted on secrecy, said to us yesterday, 'He's the very spit of Cartouche!' So much so that the detectives no longer call the mysterious robber, on the track of whom they sometimes find themselves, anything but Cartouche! Moreover the authorities, with great secrecy but with considerable intelligence—for once we find no difficulty in admitting it—have placed in the hands of three of them a history of Cartouche edited by the Librarians of the National Library. They have decided, quite subtly, that the history of Cartouche should be useful to them, not only in the matter in hand, which consists in their preventing to-day the criminal eccentricities of the new Cartouche and in arresting the new Cartouche himself, but also that his story ought to form a part of the general instruction of all detectives. Indeed a rumour has come to our ears that M. Lepine, the Prefect of Police, has ordered several of the evening courses at the Prefecture to be devoted to the authentic history of the illustrious robber."

"What do you think of that?" said Theophrastus with an air of amiable indulgence. "It's a regular farce. The journalists are queer beggars to try to stuff us with all this rubbish."

Neither Adolphe nor Marceline smiled. In a somewhat shaky voice Marceline bade him go on reading.

"The first crime of the new Cartouche, the crime at least with which the Police was first called on to occupy itself, does not present that aspect of horror which we find in some of the others. It is a romantic crime. Let us say at once that all the crimes of which we have cognisance and which are attributed to the new Cartouche, have been committed during the last fortnight and *always between eleven o'clock at night and four in the morning*."

Madame Longuet started up, her face as white as a sheet. Since the Astral operation, Theophrastus had been sleeping in the bedroom by himself, while she had slept in a small bed in the study. M. Lecamus caught her wrist and swiftly drew her back into her seat. His eyes bade her be silent.

Theophrastus paused in his reading and said, "What on earth do they mean by their new Cartouche? *Myself, I only know the old one!* . . . Well, let's hear about the romantic crime. . ."

He read on, growing calmer and calmer at every line:

"A lady, young and charming, and very well known in Paris, where her Salon is filled by all those who occupy themselves gracefully with Spiritualism—the affair is, after all, somewhat compromising, therefore we do not publish her name—was in the middle of her toilet about one o'clock in the morning, preparing to enjoy her well-earned repose after a somewhat exhausting conference with the most illustrious of the Pneumatics, when suddenly her window, which opens on to a balcony, was flung open violently, and a man of little more than middle height, still young, and extremely vigorous (this detail is in the police report), but with his hair entirely white, sprang into the room. He had in his hand a shining, nickel-plated revolver.

"'Do not be frightened, madame,' he said to the terrified lady. 'I am not going to harm you. Regard me as your most humble servant. My name is Louis-Dominique Cartouche; and my only ambition is to sup with you. By the throttle of Madame Phalaris! I've got a devil of a twist on me!' And he laughed.

"Mme. de B. . . (we will call her Mme. de B. . .) thought she had to do with a madman. But it was only a man resolved to sup with her, since, he said, he had been for a long time fascinated by her grace and charm. Yet this man was far more dangerous than a madman. For it was necessary to give way to him, *owing to his nickel-plated revolver*.

"'You are going to ring for your servants, and order them to bring an excellent supper,' said the man coolly. 'Do not give them any explanation which might cause me trouble. If you do, you're a dead woman.'

"Mme. de B. . . is a lady of courage. She rose at once to the occasion, rang for her maid, ordered supper to be brought to her boudoir, and a quarter of an hour later she and the man with the white hair were facing one another at table, *the best friends in the world*. We need hardly say that the man with the white hair made no haste over that delightful meal; and it was after two o'clock when he climbed down from the balcony. It was perhaps not unnatural that the beautiful Mme. de B. . . should not have informed the police of the adventure. It was necessity that compelled her to the avowal; for a few days later a Commissary of Police called on her, and informed her that the ring, containing a magnificent diamond, which she wore on the third finger of her right hand was the property of Mlle. Emilienne de Besançon; that that lady had seen it on her finger at a charity bazaar the day before; that Mme. de B. . . was doubtless ignorant whose property it was; doubtless it had been given to her. Mme. de B. . . was beyond words surprised and annoyed. She told the story of the balcony, the unknown, and the supper; and said that in bidding her good-bye he had forced the ring on her, saying that he had had it from a lady of whom he had been very fond, Mme. de Phalaris, *but who had died a long while ago*. It was impossible to suspect Mme. de B. . . She furnished a proof: the shining, nickel-plated revolver, which the unknown had left on a small table in the boudoir. At the same time she begged the Commissary of Police to take away a hundred bottles of champagne of the finest brands, which the unknown had sent to her the day after that extraordinary night, on the pretext that the supper had been excellent, but the champagne alone had left something to be desired. She feared lest, like the ring, the champagne should have been stolen.

"This adventure, which is the least of those we have to relate, is a faithful reproduction of an affair which took place on the night of July 13, 1721, at the house of Mme. la Maréchale de Boufflers. That lady also was at her toilet. The young man arrived by the balcony; he had not a shining, nickel-plated revolver in his hand, but he carried six English pistols in his belt. After having introduced himself as Louis-Dominique Cartouche, he demanded supper. And the widow of Louis-François, Duke de Boufflers, Peer and Marshal of France, the hero of Lille and Malplaquet, supped with Cartouche, and did not hurry over the supper.

"Cartouche only complained of the champagne; and next morning Mme. de Boufflers received a hundred bottles. He had had them taken from the cellars of a great financier by his butler Patapon.

"A few days later one of the bands of Cartouche stopped a carriage in the street. Cartouche looked in through the window and scanned the faces. It was Mme. la Maréchale de Boufflers.

"He turned to his men and said in ringing tones, 'Let Mme. la Maréchale de Boufflers pass freely to-night and always.'

"He bowed low to Mme. la Maréchale, after having slipped on her finger a magnificent diamond which he had previously stolen from Mme. de Phalaris. Mme. de Phalaris never saw it again!

"And now let us pass on to the crime in Bac Street."

XIX

The Story of the Calf

Marceline had risen and gone to her bedroom as much to hide her emotion as to ascertain whether the nickel-plated revolver was still in its drawer. When she came back into the dining-room, Theophrastus asked her what was the matter with her. Marceline replied that the revolver was no longer in its drawer. Theophrastus begged her to compose herself, and declared, in a tone which admitted of no contradiction, that since the revolver was not in its drawer, it must be somewhere else, and it was a matter of no importance whatever.

"We are now going to accompany this newspaper man to the crime in Bac Street," he went on. "His comments on the story of Mme. de B. . . , who must of course be Mme. de Bithyinie, the lady of your Pneumatic Club who is such an intimate friend of M. de la Box, show him to be a well-informed man. I am pleased to see that he does not follow those idiots of historians who try to make scandal out of my supper with Mme. la Maréchale de Boufflers, forgetting that in 1721 she was more than sixty years of age. It's a mistake that I propose to set right. My reputation might suffer from it. She was a witty and delightful talker; but I should never have dreamed, for a moment, of making love to a woman of sixty!"

As he said this, Theophrastus raised the index finger of his right hand, and waved it in the air with an authoritative gesture; and it was not Marceline or Adolphe who would have dared to contradict him.

He took up the evening paper again.

"The story of the Bac Street crime is simpler and more rapid in movement," he read. "A few days after the adventure of Mme. de B. . . the Prefect of Police received the following note: 'If you have the pluck, come and find me. I am always at Bernard's, at the café in Bac Street.' It was signed: 'Cartouche.' The Prefect pricked up his ears and laid his plans. The same evening at a quarter to twelve, half a dozen police officers dashed into the café in Bac Street. They were at once hammered with a chair by a man of extraordinary strength, still young, but with quite white hair. Three men were stretched out on the floor, and the other three had barely time to drag the three bodies of their wounded companions into the street, to save them from being burnt alive, for the man with the white hair set fire to the first storey. Then he made his escape over the roofs, springing from one roof to another over a little court, narrow indeed, but forming a kind of well more than fifty feet deep, deep enough in fact to break his neck ten times over."

"I like that," said Theophrastus, breaking off and smiling pleasantly. "Three men on the floor! I wasn't nearly so lucky in Bac Street *the other century*; for I left there nine of my lieutenants, who were arrested in spite of the massacre of the police. I thought all was lost; but one must never despair of Providence."

He took up the paper again, amid the terrified silence of M. Lecamus and Marceline, and read on:

"The new Cartouche" ("What idiots they are to keep calling him 'the new Cartouche'!") "has been also at his games in Guénégaud Street. There is in it a narrow passage crossed by a plank. Some days ago, there was found under this plank the body of a student at the Polytechnic School, M. de Bardinoldi, the mystery of whose death has so puzzled the press. What the police has confided to no one is the fact, that, pinned to the jacket of the student, was a little card on which was written in pencil: 'We shall meet again in the other world, M. de Traneuse.' There can be no doubt that this was a crime of the new Cartouche for the old one" ("One must be as stupid as a journalist," cried Theophrastus, "to suppose that there are two Cartouches!") "for the old one did in fact murder an engineer officer named M. de Traneuse on this very spot. Cartouche killed him with a blow on the back of the head with his cane; and the student had the back of his skull fractured by a blow from some blunt object."

Theophrastus stopped reading and delivered himself of some comments.

"They say to-day, 'blunt object.' Blunt object! It sounds well! Blunt object pleases me. . . You are pulling a mug," he said to Marceline and Adolphe. "And you're holding on to one another as if you expected some catastrophe. It's silly to lose your hair about a few practical jokes. I profit by the occasion, my dear Adolphe, to explain to you the pleasure I take in frequenting Guénégaud Street. This business of M. de Traneuse was the origin of one of the best tricks I ever played on M. d'Argenson's police officers. After the execution of M. de Traneuse, who had permitted himself to make some extremely disagreeable remarks about me, I was pursued by two patrols of the watch, who surrounded me and rendered resistance impossible. But they did not know that I was Cartouche, and contented themselves with conducting me to Fort-L'Eveque, the least severe prison in Paris, where they shut up debtors, disorderly actors, and people who had not paid fines. It was only on the 10th of January that they knew that they had captured Cartouche; but on the evening of the 9th Cartouche had escaped and resumed the direction of his Police. It was time, for everything was topsy-turvy in the streets of Paris. My dear Marceline, and you too, Adolphe, you look as if you were going to a funeral. And yet this article doesn't lack *a certain salt*. I thought at first it was a scribbler's joke, but I see that it is quite serious. It is really: take it from me. And wait for the story of the calf! We have only got to the affair of Petits-Augustins Street. . . Listen."

Theophrastus raised the evening paper again, adjusted his gold-rimmed spectacles on his nose, and went on:

"The most incredible thing in this extraordinary story is that several times during the last week the police have been on the very point of catching the modern Cartouche, and that he has always escaped by the chimney, just like *the other*. History teaches us that that was the practice of the real Cartouche. On the 11th of June, 1721, he had formed the plan of robbing Desmarets House, Petits-Augustins Street. It was one of his men, the Ratlet, who had suggested the coup to him. But the Police had their eye on Cartouche and the Ratlet; and no sooner were they in Desmarets House than the archers rushed to the spot, and the house was surrounded. Cartouche had the doors of the rooms quietly locked and the lights put out. He undressed himself, climbed up the chimney, descended by another chimney into the kitchen, where he found a scullion. He killed the scullion, dressed himself in his clothes, and walked out of the house, shooting down with his pistols two archers, who asked him where Cartouche was. Well, what will you say when we tell you that yesterday our Cartouche, having been tracked to a confectioner's in the Augustins Quarter, escaped by the chimney, after having put on over his own clothes, which doubtless he desired to keep clean, the over-alls of the confectioner, which were found on the roof? As for the confectioner he was found, half cooked, in his own oven. But before putting him into it, Cartouche had taken the precaution of previously assassinating him."

Here Theophrastus once more broke off his reading.

"Previously!" he cried. "Previously! These journalists are marvellous! . . . I had *previously* assassinated him! . . . But why have you gone into the corner? Am I frightening you? Come, come, my dear

Marceline; come, Adolphe: a little coolness. You'll want it for the story of the calf!"

"Never," says Theophrastus in his memoirs, which from this epoch become deeply tinged with a vast melancholy, "never before had either my wife or M. Lecamus worn such expressions at the reading of a mere newspaper article. But if we let ourselves be frightened by everything the newspapers tell us, we should *be for ever on the rack*. The journalists describe the events of the day with a particularly surprising power of imagination in the matter of crime. They must have their daily blood. It is indeed laughable. A knife-thrust more or less costs them nothing; and they only make me shrug my shoulders. The knife-thrusts of these gentlemen do not trouble my digestion in the slightest; and, I repeat, I shrug my shoulders at them.

"When I came to the place in the article at which Cartouche put the baker's man in the oven, my wife groaned as heavily as if that baker's man had been her brother; and leaving her chair, she shrank back little by little into the left-hand corner of the dining-room, nearest the hall. M. Lecamus was in a position quite as ridiculous. He had retired to the right-hand corner of the dining-room, nearest the hall. They were staring at me as if they were staring at a phenomenon at a fair, an eater of live rabbits, or something of that kind. I was displeased; I did not conceal from them my opinion that such childish behaviour was unworthy of two reasonable beings; and with some severity I begged them to return to their places by my side. But they did not do so. Then I started on the story of 'The Calf's Revenge.'

"I read:

"'M. Houdry is a butcher on the outer Boulevard. His specialty is veal; and people come from all parts of the district to purchase it. His renown is explained by a fact so exceptional that we should have refused to believe it, except for the repeated declarations of the Commissary of Police, M. Mifroid, who held the first inquiry into the circumstances of the crime. It is well known that the Paris butchers receive their meat from public slaughter-houses, and are forbidden to have slaughter-houses of their own. But every day M. Houdry killed a calf at home!'

"'That's quite right,' I said. 'M. Houdry explained it to me several times; and I was rather surprised at the confidence he showed in me when he told me about his mysterious slaughter-house. Why should he have revealed to me a fact which was known only to his wife, his assistant, a foundling whom he reckoned as one of the family, and to his brother-in-law who every night brought the calf? Why? There is no telling. Perhaps it was stronger than he! You know well that *one never escapes one's destiny*. I used to say to him: "Take care! It will end by the calves getting to know about it."'

"I went on with my reading:

"'This calf was brought to him *in silence* every night by his brother-in-law; and since the little back-yard in which his slaughter-house is situated looks out on some waste land behind, no one ever saw a live calf at M. Houdry's house. M. Houdry attached so much importance to killing his calves himself because his veal owed its excellence to his manner of killing it.'

"'As a matter of fact,' I broke off to say, 'he used to cut off their heads at a single blow, with a big cutlass.'

"'Early yesterday morning M. Houdry shut himself up as usual in his slaughter-house, with his calf. His assistant helped him tie up the calf. As a rule, M. Houdry took from twenty-five to thirty minutes preparing his veal for the stall. Thirty-five minutes passed; and the double doors of the slaughter-house did not open. Sometimes M. Houdry called his assistant to help him finish the work. That morning he did not call him. Forty minutes passed. Then Mme. Houdry, the butcher's wife, came to the back door and said to the assistant: "What's your master doing this morning? He's a long time over his work."

"'"Yes; much longer than usual," said the assistant.

"'Then she called, "Houdry! Houdry!" There was no answer; and she walked across the back-yard, and opened the doors of the slaughter-house. At once the calf ran out and began to dance gracefully round her. (Dear! dear! I begin to dread some great misfortune!) She looked at the calf with some surprise, for at that hour the calf should have been veal. Then she opened the door wider, and called to her husband. He did not answer; she turned towards his assistant and said:

"'"Your master isn't here. Are you sure he hasn't gone out?"

"'"Quite sure, Mum. I've been in the back-yard all the time. I expect he's hiding behind the door to jump out and give you a fright, Mum. You know what a joker the master is. But all the same, *he'd much better be hiding the calf*. If anybody sees it, he'll get into trouble."

"'So saying, he sprang at the head of the calf and slipped a halter over it.

"'"Houdry! Houdry!" cried his wife. "You're hiding to give me a fright! Don't be silly!"

"'There was no answer; and she went into the slaughter-house. Then she screamed; she had found M. Houdry. He was not hiding at all.

"'*He was laid out, in neat joints of veal, on the table.*'

"'I told him so,' said I. 'I told him so more than once. My presentiments always come true. I expected some great misfortune! And here it is! Every day, again and again, I told M. Houdry to look out: that one does not kill so many calves without the calves getting to know about it. But he always laughed at me. Yet the Theory of Chances always confronts us. It confronted him. He took no notice of it. He took no notice of anything: neither of the way the calf looked at him, nor of the Theory of Chances. But I said to him: "My dear M. Houdry, if a butcher can kill more than a thousand calves in Paris, when it is forbidden by the law, there will certainly be found one calf to kill the butcher!" And here you are! The calf has cut up the butcher! Well, well, it's nobody's fault. . . Let us continue this interesting article.'

"'Mme. Houdry screamed and fainted. The butcher boy also screamed and fainted—he was a foundling. A few minutes later the drama was discovered. One can imagine the emotion of the neighbourhood. . .' (There was reason for it. Poor M. Houdry: he was a fine fellow. And now they will have to try the calf. The calf will be a great success in the dock. It's a strange, fantastic, inexorable, and courageous calf!)

"The journalist was not of the opinion that the calf had cut up the butcher. And once more he dragged in the name of Cartouche. (Poor old Cartouche!) Once more I shrugged my shoulders. Then, raising my eyes above the top of the paper, I looked into the two corners of the drawing-room for those two foolish creatures who had so childishly retired to them—my wife and M. Lecamus. I looked in vain. They had disappeared. I called to them loudly. They did not answer. I hunted through the flat without finding them. Then I tried to open the door on to the landing; but it would not open. They had locked me in.

"That did not trouble me at all. When I am locked in, I go out by the chimneys, if they are big enough; if they are too small, I leave by the window. But my drawing-room chimney is a monumental chimney; there is not another like it in Gerando Street; and I climbed up it with the same ease with which I had climbed down the chimney of M. Houdry on the very morning on which the calf cut up that excellent but unfortunate man! I soon came out on to the roof into a very cold and rainy night which filled me with a profound sadness."

XX

The Strange Behaviour of an Express Train

That profound sadness was destined to affect seriously the future of Theophrastus. As he made his way over the roofs of Gerando Street, it increased to such a paralysing intensity that presently he sat down on the edge of a roof, with his legs dangling over the street, and plunged into the bitterest reflections. The result of this unwise action was that he caught a severe cold.

As he sat reflecting, he slowly came to himself, his modern self. During the reading of the article which narrated the crimes of the new Cartouche, he had displayed a carelessness airy to the point of callousness. Now the sense of his responsibility, especially in the matter of cutting up the butcher Houdry, weighed on him more and more heavily. The memory of many midnight outings, by way of the chimney he had just climbed, came into his mind; and several sanguinary crimes filled his blinking eyes with the too tardy tears of an ineffectual remorse.

So, in spite of all the suffering he had endured, in spite of all the passionate prayers of M. de la Nox to Æon, Source of Æons, *Cartouche was not dead; the Black Feather ever sprouted afresh*. This very night, as on so many other nights of crime, he was out on the roofs of Paris with his familiar spirit and his Black Feather. He wept. He cursed that mysterious and irresistible force which, from the depth of the centuries, bade him slay. He cursed the gesture which slays. He thought of his wife and his friend. He recalled with bitter regret the hours of happiness passed with those dear ones. He forgave them their terror and their flight. He resolved never again henceforth to trouble their peaceful hours with his red vagaries.

"Let us vanish!" said he. "Let us hide our shame and our original obliquity in the heart of the desert! They will forget me! . . . I shall forget myself! Let us profit by these *moments of reason* in which my brain, for the while free from the Past, discusses, weighs, deduces, and forms conclusions in the *Present*. It is no longer Cartouche who speaks. To-night it is Theophrastus who wills! Theophrastus who cries to Cartouche: 'Let us fly! let us fly! Since I love Marceline, let us fly! Since I love Adolphe, let us fly! One day they will be happy without thee; with thee there is no longer any happiness! . . . Farewell! Farewell, Marceline, beloved wife! Farewell, Adolphe, dear friend and comforter! . . . Farewell! Theophrastus bids you farewell!'"

He wept and wept. Then he said aloud:

"Come along, Cartouche."

He plunged into the night, springing from gutter to gutter, crawling from roof to roof, sliding from the tops of walls with the ease, the balance, and the sureness of a somnambulist.

And now, who is this man who, with bowed head and stooping back, his hands in his pockets, wanders like Fortune's step-son through the bitter wind and the rain that falls all the dreary way? He moves along the road which runs beside the railway, a road dismally straight, bordered by dismal little stunted trees, the dismal ornaments of the departmental road, the road which runs beside the railway. Whence does this man, or rather this shadow of a man, this sad shadow of a man, with his hands in his pockets, come? On his right and on his left stretches the plain, without an undulation, without the bulge of a hill, without the hollow of a river—stretches grey and gloomy under the grey and gloomy sky.

Now and again along the railway, so painfully straight, trains pass,—slow trains, express trains, freight trains. While they pass the railway snores; then it is silent, and one hears, borne on the wind, the ting-ting-ting-ting of the little electric bell in the little railway station in front. But what little railway station? There is one in front; there is one behind. They are three miles apart; and between them the double line of rails runs as straight as a die. Between the two railway stations there are no viaducts, no tunnel, no bridge, not even a level-crossing. I dwell on these details on account of the strange behaviour of the express train.

That sad shadow of a man is Theophrastus. He has resolved to fly, to fly no matter where, from his wife—poor dear, unfortunate, heroic fellow! After a night passed on the roofs of Paris, not knowing whither to direct his steps, yet not wishing to stay them, he went into a railway station—what railway station? Shall we ever know?—And without a ticket he got on a train, and without a ticket somewhere he got off it and came out of another railway station. It may be that in this evasion of the duties of the passenger his Black Feather stood him in good stead.

Behold him then on the road. . . At the entrance to a village. . . On the road which runs beside the railway.

Whom does he perceive on the threshold of a cottage at the entrance to the village? . . . The Signora Petito herself!

It was the first time the Signora Petito had seen M. Longuet since he clipped her husband's ears. She fell into a fury. She ran down to the garden gate; and her anger found vent not only in abuse, but in the most imprudent revelations. Had Signor Petito heard what his angry Regina said, he would have smacked her for her incredible folly. After abusing Theophrastus for his barbarity to Signor Petito, she told him with vindictive triumph that her husband had found the treasures of the Chopinettes, and that those treasures were the richest in the world, treasures worth far more than a couple of ears, were they as big as the ears of Signor Petito. "They are quits!"

In the course of this outburst, Theophrastus with considerable difficulty interjected a few words; but he was not at all disturbed by it. Indeed he was grateful to the fury of Signora Petito for having given him such important information. He said grimly:

"*I shall find my treasures, for I shall find Signor Petito.*"

The Signora Petito burst into a satanic laugh, and cried:

"Signor Petito is in the train!"

"In what train?"

"*In the train which is going to pass under your nose.*"

"What is the train which is going to pass under my nose?"

"The train which is carrying my husband beyond the frontier! Get into it, M. Longuet! Get into it if you want to speak to Signor Petito. But you'd better make haste, for it passes in less than an hour, and you can't buy a ticket for it at any of these little stations. *It doesn't stop at them!*"

She laughed an even more satanic laugh, so satanic that Theophrastus longed for the moments when he was deaf. He raised his hat, and went quickly down the road which runs beside the railway. When he was alone, between the little trees and the telegraph posts, he said to himself:

"Come, come! I must ask news of my treasures of Signor Petito himself. . . But how the deuce am I to do it? He is in the train *which is going to pass under my nose.*"

At this point it is necessary to give a map:

Station A D C Station B.

x———x——x——x

It is unnecessary to give the names of the stations, for the demonstration is practically geometrical, and to geometry letters are more appropriate.

Let us go to station A. The signal-man of station A hears the *ting!* of the bell which announces that the express he is expecting has passed station B, and is on that section of the block-system which begins at station A and ends at station B. The express goes from B to A. It is on the line B A. That is clear. The signal at A announces the train by lowering its little red arm with a *ting!*

The signal-man at station A waits for the train, and waits for the train, and waits for the train! It ought to be there. It is a train which goes sixty miles an hour, and, if it is late, it goes seventy or eighty. The distance between station A and station B is at the most three miles and a furlong. Three minutes and a half is the longest an express takes to do the distance. The signal-man, frightened to death at not seeing the train appear, shouts to the station-master that the train ought to have gone through! The station-master dashes to the telegraph, and telegraphs station B: "Train signalled not arrived!" Station B answers: "Joker!" Station A: "It's serious. What are we to do? Horrible anxiety." Station B: "Notify Jericho!" Station A: "There must have been an accident! We are hurrying along the line! Come and meet us!" Station B: "What can have happened? We are coming."

Then the station-master, the porters, and the ticket-clerks of stations A and B hurry along the line, the staff of station A going towards station B, the staff of station B going towards station A. They hurry along, in the full light of day, in the middle of a perfectly flat plain, a plain without a river, without ridge, and without hollow. They hurry along the line, and meet one another between A and B. . . But they do not meet the train!

The station-master of station A (I say particularly of station A), who suffered from heart disease, fell down dead.

XXI

The Earless Man with His Head Out of the Window

Let us state this geometrical problem in the simplest words: an express train has to cover the ground between two little stations three miles apart. It is announced at the second when it passes the first; and yet they wait for it at the second in vain. They hurry from both stations down the line to find the wreck; but they do not so much as find the train, an express train in which there are perhaps a hundred passengers.

That the station-master of A should have fallen down dead at the shock of this unheard-of, bewildering, stupefying, absurd, diabolical, and yet how simple (as we shall learn later) disappearance of the train, is not greatly to be wondered at. The minds of all of them were shaken by the occurrence. The station-master of B was not in a much better condition than his colleague. Everyone present uttered incoherent cries. They kept calling the train, as if the train could have answered! They did not hear it, and on that flat plain they did not see it! The ticket-clerk of station A knelt down beside the body of his chief, and presently said, "I am quite sure he is dead!" The rest gathered round the body of the dead man; and then, tearing up two of the little trees from the side of the road which runs beside the railway, they laid him on them. Carrying the body on this rude litter, they returned towards station A. We must bear in mind that the express had passed station B, and that no one had seen it reach station A.

But they had not yet reached station A when, on the line, *on the line along which they had just come*, they perceived a railway-carriage, or rather a railway-carriage and a guard's-van! They greeted the sight in their excitable French way with the howls of madmen. Where did this end of a train come from? And what had become of the beginning of the train, that is to say, of the engine, the tender, the dining-car, and the three corridor carriages?

Look at the plan. C marks the point on the line at which the staffs of stations A and B met, when they were hunting for the train. It is also the point at which the station-master of A fell down dead. The two staffs then, in a body, were bringing back the dead station-master towards A, when at the point D, a point they had passed a few minutes before, and at which they had seen nothing, they find a railway-carriage and a guard's-van.

These people greeted this sight with the cries of madmen; and then they perceived an odd-looking head looking out of one of the windows of the railway-carriage. It waggled. This head had no ears; and the earless man *had his head out of the carriage window*. They shouted to him. From the moment they caught sight of him they asked him what had happened. But the man did not answer. The odd thing was that his head waggled from left to right, as if it were moved by the wind which was blowing at the time with some force. It was a head with crinkly hair. It was bent downwards; and the cravat round a high collar, very white on that grey day, was untied and streaming in the wind.

At last when they came quite near (they moved slowly owing to the fact that they were carrying the station-master) they saw clearly the shocking reality. The man not only had his head out of the window, he had also got it caught in the window. The unfortunate wretch must have opened the window and stuck his head out while the train was in motion; and the window must have been jerked up violently and cut his head half off! On seeing this, the two staffs howled afresh; then they set down the body of the station-master, ran round the guard's-van, *in which there was nobody*, and opening a door on the other side of the carriage, they found that it was empty, except for the man *whose head was caught in the window*, and that his body, inside the carriage, was *stripped of every rag of clothing*.

The news of these fantastic horrors at once spread throughout the district. An enormous crowd thronged the platforms of station A all the rest of the day. The chief officials of the line came from Paris. Not only were they unable to explain, on that day and the days following, the death of the man who had had his head out of the carriage window, but they were still unable to find either the train or the passengers. They talked of nothing but this strange affair at the funeral of the station-master of A, which was celebrated with great solemnity, and also throughout Europe and America.

XXII

In Which the Catastrophe Which Appears on the Point of Being Explained, Grows Yet More Inexplicable

So far I have only given the simplest plan of the line that I might get the basis of the affair as clear as possible. That plan is not quite complete, for though there was only this one line joining the stations A and B there was a short side-line, H I, which led to a sand-pit which had supplied a glass-factory. But since the glass-factory had failed, they no longer worked the sand-pit; and the side-line was practically abandoned. Here is the complete plan:

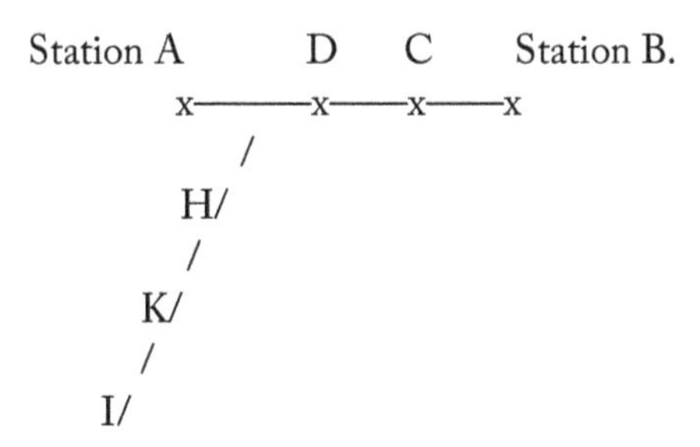

It will naturally be supposed that this side-line leading to the sand-pit is going to provide the explanation, the quite simple explanation of the disappearance of the express. But if the matter had been as simple as the side-line would appear to make it, I should hardly have omitted it from the first map. I could have said at once: "It is quite clear that, owing to a train of circumstances which it remains to determine, the express, instead of continuing to follow the line B A, must have turned off up the side-line H I, and buried itself in the vast mass of loose sand at the sand-pit I. Rushing along at a speed of over sixty miles an hour, it evidently plunged into the mass of sand, which covered it up; and that is the stupid but actual reason of its disappearance."

But, to say nothing of the fact that this does not explain the presence, at the point D, of the guard's-van and railway-carriage, out of the window of which Signor Petito had stuck his head, this explanation could not have failed to occur to the alert intelligence of the engineers of the company. Moreover, there were points and a switch at the point H; this switch, in accordance with the rules, was padlocked; and the key had been taken away.

I indeed attached no importance to the fact that *the padlock was locked*; for, it seemed to me quite probable that the key had been left in the padlock, *which had actually been the case*, and that Theophrastus, who had good reasons for stopping the train in order to join Signor Petito, had profited by the presence of that key, to shift the points. It was only a matter of thrusting over the lever of the switch; and that would explain why the train was not seen by the signal-man at A, since, instead of continuing along the line B A, it had turned off up H I towards the sand-pit. I told myself all this; and if it had explained anything, I should have stated it at once, and instead of giving two maps I should have given merely the latter with the side-line H I on it.

That I have not done so is owing to the fact that the side-line H I explains nothing. I also believed at first that it was going to make the disappearance of the express clear to us, but as a matter of fact *it complicates the catastrophe instead of explaining it*; for here is the story, the true story; and that too continues to explain nothing at all.

Wandering along the road which runs beside the railway, Theophrastus had noticed the little side-line, and seen that the key had been left in the padlock of the switch. This fact, which had been of no importance to him before his brief but stormy interview with Signora Petito, assumed an enormous importance when he resolved to join, at any cost, Signor Petito, who was in the train *which was about to pass under his nose*. M. Longuet said to himself: "I cannot board the express, rushing between the two stations A and B, in the usual way. But there is a little side-line H I, the key is in the padlock of the switch; I have only to turn the lever, and the express will dash up H I. Since it is broad daylight the engine-driver will see what has happened, he will stop the train, and I shall take advantage of its stopping to board it."

Nothing could be more simple; and Theophrastus did it. He dragged over the lever of the switch, walked up the side-line, and waited for the express.

Theophrastus, hidden behind a tree that none of the officials on the express might see him, awaited its coming at the point K, that is to say, rather more than half-way up the side-line, that is to say, *on this side of the sand-pit I*. He waited for the express coming from H, *with his eyes on the track.* If, as everyone must have been supposing ever since I mentioned the sand-pit, the train coming from H had buried itself in the sand at I, Theophrastus, who was at K, between H and I, must have seen it. But Theophrastus waited for the train and waited for the train and waited for the train. He waited for it as the signal-man at station A had waited for it; and he no more saw the express than did the signal-man at A and the rest of the officials of the line.

The express had disappeared for M. Longuet as it had disappeared for the rest of the world.

So much so that, tired of waiting, M. Longuet walked down as far as H to see what was happening. There he saw the staff of A, which was hurrying towards B in its search for the express. He asked himself sadly what could have become of the express; and finding no answer to the question, he walked up H I, and when he arrived at K, which he had just left, he found the empty guard's-van and the railway-carriage which a few minutes later the two staffs were to find at D!

Once more he swore by the throttle of Mme. Phalaris, and buried his brow in his hands, asking himself how that guard's-van and that carriage came to be there, since the express itself had not come. *It had not come, since he, Theophrastus, had not quitted the track.*

Suddenly he saw the head of a man waggling out of the window of the railway-carriage; and since this head had no ears, he recognised Signor Petito.

He sprang up into the railway-carriage, *and without troubling to let down the window and release the head* of the unfortunate expert in handwriting, he stripped him of his clothes, and proceeded to put them on. Theophrastus, who knew himself to be tracked by the police and in whom the astuteness of Cartouche sprang to life again, was disguising himself. When he was dressed, he made a bundle of his own clothes, and descended from the carriage. He felt in Signor Petito's pockets, took out his pocket-book, sat down on the embankment, and plunged into the study of the papers it contained, hunting for the traces of his treasures. But Signor Petito had carried to the tomb the secret of the treasures of the Chopinettes; never again were the Gall, the Cock, the Chopinettes, or the treasures to be discussed: with the result that Signora Petito, who learnt a few minutes later of the extraordinary death of her husband, presently went mad, and was confined in a lunatic asylum for six months.

But we are only concerned with the misfortune of Theophrastus, which so surpasses all other human misfortunes, and which is so hard to believe that we need all the assistance that Science can give us to credit it wholly. I cannot believe that the minds of my readers are so base, or their imaginations so poor, that the matter of the treasures could be of any genuine interest to them, when they are confronted by this phenomenon, of such surpassing interest, the soul of Theophrastus.

Presently that unfortunate man, on failing to find anything of interest to him in the papers of Signor Petito, heaved a deep sigh. He raised his head; and lo! *the guard's-van and the railway-carriage of Signor Petito had disappeared*!

XXIII

The Melodious Bricklayer

Theophrastus, though he had with good reason made up his mind never again to be astonished by anything, was nevertheless astonished by the disappearance of the railway-carriage, with the earless head of Signor Petito waggling in the wind. With a melancholy air he walked down the little side-line, asking himself whether he ought to be more astonished by the disappearance of the carriage than by its sudden appearance. In truth, the suppression of the express was troubling his spirit deeply.

It seems to me that I, who know the secrets of the sandalwood box, have no right to give the explanation of this suppression before the hour at which Theophrastus learnt it himself, from a quite commonplace observation which the Commissary of Police, M. Mifroid, an earnest student of Logic from his earliest years, made to him in the Catacombs of Paris. At the same time, it is only fair to say that all the points in the problem are already in the possession of the reader, who can solve it himself, if indeed he has not already done so, without further delay. Theophrastus then, in a state of prostration, walked down the side-line, arrived at the bifurcation, examined the switch, thrust back the lever which he had thrust over, locked the padlock, and carried away, once and for all, the key which had been so carelessly left in it a few days before. He performed this action because he felt that it was only right; and he restored the switch to its place, because he felt that his reason could not stand another disappearance of the express.

Still melancholy, he reached the deserted station A. All the rest of the staff was absent on the search for the express; only the signal-man was on the look-out. Theophrastus questioned the signal-man, who could only say, as he pointed to the red arm of the signal:

"*The express is signalled, but it does not come!*"

"Was it really signalled from the last station?" said Theophrastus.

"Yes, sir, the station-master and all the staff of the last station saw the express go through it. They telegraphed it to us. Besides, sir, look at my little red arm! Look at my little red arm! And it is quite impossible that there should have been a wreck between the last station and this one.

There is no bridge, sir, no viaduct, no works of art. Besides, just now I climbed to the top of that ladder against the big tank there. From it you can see the whole line right to the other station. I saw our people down the line, gesticulating, but I did not see the express!"

"Strange—very strange," said Theophrastus mournfully.

"Strange isn't the word for it! Look at my little red arm!"

"Inexplicable!" said Theophrastus gloomily.

"The most inexplicable thing in the world!" cried the signal-man.

"Not so: there is one thing even more inexplicable than an express which disappears with its engine and passengers without anyone being able to tell what has become of it," said Theophrastus in the same gloomy tone.

"What on earth's that?" said the signal-man, opening his astonished eyes wider than ever.

"Why, a railway-carriage without an engine which suddenly appears without one's being able to tell where it comes from."

"What?" cried the signal-man.

"And which disappeared as suddenly as it appeared. . . You haven't by any chance seen a railway-carriage with a man looking out of the window pass this way?"

"You're laughing at me, sir!" said the signal-man with some heat. "*You're exaggerating!* Just because you don't believe the story of the express which has been signalled and does not come! But look, sir, look! Look at my little red arm!"

M. Longuet replied: "If you haven't seen the express, no more have I!"

He shrugged his shoulders bitterly and left the station. An idea had occurred to him: his misfortune was so utter and so irremediable that he was resolved to die. . . for others.

With a little astuteness the thing is practicable, even easy. Since he is dressed in the clothes of Signor Petito, nothing prevents him leaving his own clothes on the bank of the first river he comes to. This simple proceeding will constitute a formal act of suicide. Behold Marceline and Adolphe once more at peace!

On the bank of what river did M. Longuet lay his clothes? How did he re-enter Paris? These are matters of such little importance that he makes no mention of them in his memoirs. There is only one thing that is really important, *the explanation of the disappearance of the express*.

In the dull November sunset a workman was bricking up a hole in the roadway of a Paris square in the ancient Quarter d'Enfer. As he filled it he was singing the *Internationale*, the hymn of the advanced Labour Parties throughout the world.

This workman, a bricklayer, was with his comrades engaged in assisting in that perpetual occupation of modern municipalities, getting the streets up; and the street was up.

The municipal engineers had been making a new sewer through the Quarter d'Enfer with a patient disregard of the fact that under that quarter the Catacombs spread their innumerable tunnels. It was but natural that the bottom of the end of the excavation, in which they were laying the new sewer, should have fallen out, and that they should have been obliged to rest the pipes on railway sleepers cut in half. They were, however, at the end of their task: the hole at the bottom of the excavation, which ran right down to a passage of the Catacombs, had been nearly bricked up; and the aperture which remained could not have been much more than three feet across. As the bricklayer bricked it up, he sang the *Internationale*.

At the same hour, a few yards down the side of the square, M. Mifroid stood before the counter of a shop at which they sold electric lamps, and was buying half a dozen of them for his men. Each lamp was guaranteed to give forty-eight hours' light, though they were not much larger than cigar-cases. His lamps had been packed up; and he had just put his fingers through the loop of the string of the packet, when a little way down the counter he perceived a man, still young but with quite white hair, slipping several examples of these electric lamps into his pocket without paying for them. They would doubtless be quite as useful to a thief as a policeman. M. Mifroid, with his usual courage, sprang towards the man, crying, "It's Cartouche!"

He had recognised him owing to the fact that since the Calf's Revenge every Commissary of Police in Paris carried a portrait of the new Cartouche in his pocket. They owed them to Mme. Longuet herself and M. Lecamus, who had fled from the article in the evening paper to the nearest police-station, since they felt themselves bound, in the interests of humanity, to inform the police, somewhat tardily, of the bicentenary mental condition of Theophrastus.

Therefore M. Mifroid, who had had the further advantage of a passing acquaintance with Theophrastus in his home, recognised him at once.

Theophrastus, who had for some nights known the intentions of the police, when he saw M. Mifroid and heard his cry, said to himself, "It's time I was off!"

He bolted out of the shop; and the Commissary of Police bolted after him.

To return to our bricklayer, he sang the *Internationale* all the time. He was alone, because his comrades had gone round the corner to refresh themselves. He was at the chorus of the song; and it was the seventy-ninth time he had sung it since two o'clock in the afternoon. He raised his head towards Heaven and roared:

"Cellalutte finale
Groupppons-nous etddemain. . ."

With his head turned to Heaven he did not see two shadows flying headlong, which, one after the other, fell through the hole; their cries were drowned in the volume of sound which poured from his lungs. They were the shadows of Theophrastus and of M. Mifroid pursuing him through the dusk. In their careless haste they fell clean through the street which was up. The bricklayer turned his head a little to the right and roared enthusiastically:

"L'Interrrnationaaaaleu
Sera le genrrhummain! . . ."

And he finished bricking up the hole. Singing the *Internationale*, he had performed the symbolic act of interring a policeman and a thief.

XXIV

The Solution in the Catacombs

When one comes to oneself in the depth of the Catacombs," says Commissary Mifroid in the admirable report of the matter which he drew up, "the first thought which steals into one's mind is a fearful one: the fear of being old-fashioned. I mean by that a sudden anxiety lest one should find oneself reproducing all the ridiculous behaviour of which writers of romance and melodrama never fail to make their unfortunate heroes guilty when they find themselves immured in caves, grottoes, excavations, caverns, or tombs.

"At the moment of my fall, even while I was so rapidly covering the space which separated me from the soil of the Catacombs, my presence of mind did not forsake me. I was aware that I was falling into those thousand-year-old subways which interlace their innumerable and capricious windings under the soil of Paris. The next thing I was aware of was a slight and painful numbness which followed my recovery from the insensibility into which I had been plunged by the inevitable shock. I was, then, in the Catacombs. At once I said to myself, 'Above all things I must not be old-fashioned.'

"It would have been old-fashioned, for example, to utter cries of despair, to appeal to Providence, or to strike my brow against the wall of the passage. It would have been old-fashioned to find at the bottom of my pocket a bar of chocolate and at once divide it into eight pieces which would have represented assured sustenance for eight days. It would have been equally old-fashioned to find a candle-end in my pocket—a place in which no rational human being ever keeps candle-ends—and five or six matches, and so create the harrowing problem whether one ought to let the candle burn once it was lighted, or blow it out and rekindle it at the cost of another match, a problem which often interferes with the digestions of whole families who read romances.

"I had nothing in my pocket. I assured myself of the fact with extreme satisfaction; and in the darkness of the Catacombs I slapped my pockets, repeating: 'Nothing! Nothing! Nothing!'

"At the same moment it occurred to me that it would be quite up-to-date for a man in my situation to illuminate without further delay the opaque darkness which weighed so heavily on my eyes and tired them, with a sudden and radiant electric star. Had I not, before falling into this hole, bought half a dozen electric lamps of the latest pattern? The parcel must have accompanied me in my fall. Without stirring I groped about and laid my hand on it. By great good luck the lamps were unbroken; I took one of them and pressed the button. The excavation was lighted by a fairy glow; and I could not refrain from smiling at the unfortunate wretch who, shut up in some cavern, invariably crawls along, holding his breath, behind a miserable little flame which presently he hurriedly blows out.

"I rose to my feet, and examined the ceiling. I had known that the streets were up, and that the work was nearly finished. I was the less surprised therefore, on looking up through the hole through which I had fallen, to see no spark of daylight, and to realise that it had been quite bricked up. Now several yards of earth separated me from living creatures, without the slightest possibility of my boring through them, even if the ceiling had not been far too high for me to reach. I satisfied myself of this without any feeling of annoyance; then, having turned my electric ray on the floor, I perceived a body.

"It was the body of M. Theophrastus Longuet, the body of the new Cartouche. I examined it and perceived that it showed no signs of any serious injury. The man must be stunned, as I had been myself; and doubtless he would presently recover. I called to mind the fact that M. Lecamus had introduced me to his friend one day in the Champs-Elysées; and here I was face to face with him as one of the most abandoned of assassins.

"Even as this flashed into my mind, M. Longuet heaved a deep sigh, and stretched out his arms. He complained of pains about his body, bade me good-evening, and asked me where we were. I told him. He did not appear utterly dismayed by the information, but drawing a pocket-book from his pocket, he traced some lines which looked like a plan, showed them to me, and said:

"'My dear M. Mifroid, we are in the depths of the Catacombs. It's an extraordinary event; and how we are to get out I do not know. But the matter which fills my mind at this moment is really far more interesting, believe me, than falling into the Catacombs. I beg you to glance at this little plan.'

"He handed me the leaf from his pocket-book, on which I saw the following:

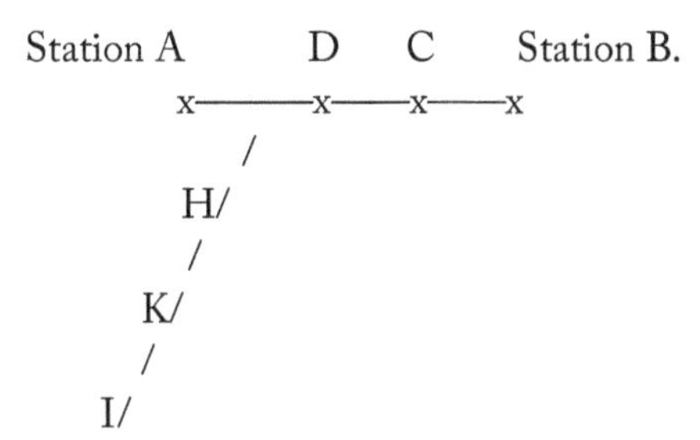

"He sneezed twice.

"'Oh, you have a cold,' said I, taking the paper.

"'Yes; I have had a bad cold since taking a somewhat long stroll one rainy night on the roofs of Gerando Street,' he said.

"I advised him not to neglect it. I must say that this quiet and natural conversation between two men in the depths of the Catacombs, a few minutes after their recovery from such an unexpected fall, gave me infinite pleasure. Having considered the lines on the paper, I asked the explanation of them; and M. Longuet told me the story of the disappearance of an express train and of the reappearance of a railway-carriage, which was by far the most fantastic I had ever heard. This man had desired to make an express disappear between A and B by sending it up a side-line H I, by shifting the points, *and he had waited for it at K*. But the train had neither appeared at A nor at K, that is to say, either to him or to anyone else. Next a railway-carriage had appeared to him at K; and presently that railway-carriage itself had disappeared. I could well have believed that this man, considering his past (the past of Cartouche!) and the story which he now told me, was mad, if he had not expressed himself so logically, and given me the most exact material details about the points, the switch, and all the facts of the case.

"Moreover, it is a matter of common experience that a madman always understands everything. But this man wanted to understand. I begged him to repeat the story. He said nothing. Twice I reiterated the request and still he said nothing. I was about to lose patience, when, grasping the fact that I had asked him something, he told me that now and then he was deaf for a few minutes.

"Since he had recovered his hearing, we returned to the problem of the express. He assured me that he would rather die ten times in the depths of the Catacombs than come out of them once without knowing what had become of this express. 'I do not wish,' he added, 'to lose the most precious thing in the world: my Reason.'

"'And when did this happen?' said I. 'For, as a matter of fact, I have heard nothing of the disappearance of an express; and it ought to be generally known.'

"'It must be known by now,' he, said in a very melancholy tone. 'It only happened a few hours before our fall into the Catacombs.'

"I examined the paper once more for quite five minutes. I reflected deeply, asked for certain complementary details, and then burst out laughing: though in truth it was not a laughable matter, for the catastrophe was truly appalling. What made me laugh was the seeming difficulty of the problem and the delight of having solved it in five minutes.

"'You believe yourself a rational human being,' I cried, 'because you have Reason! But you're exactly like ninety-nine people out of a hundred, you don't know how to make use of it. You talk of Reason; *but what use is Reason in a brain which does not know by which end to take hold of it*? It's a wonderful instrument in the hands of a doll! Don't turn away your head in that sulky way, M. Longuet. I tell you: *you don't know by which end to take hold of your Reason!* Come, M. Longuet: let us reason with this paper in our hands.'

"He tried, the duffer! He said: 'There were five men at A, and five men at B. The five men at B saw the train pass; the five men at A did not see it. I—I was at K; and I am sure that it did not pass at K. . . consequently. . .'

"'Consequently? . . . Consequently, there's no longer any express? Consequently your express has vanished—melted—flown away? Hey, presto: vanish express! *You think perhaps that the express is in the English Channel!* You see clearly, M. Longuet, that if you have Reason, you don't know how to use it. Allow me to tell you *that you took hold of your Reason by the wrong end!* The wrong end is that which begins by saying, 'We did not see the express,' and which ends by saying, 'Then there is no longer any express!' But I am going *to show you how to take hold of your Reason by the right end*. It is this: the truth is that the express exists, and that it exists between the points B, where it was seen to pass, A, where it was not seen to pass, and I, where it could not pass. Since we are in a plain, your express is between A, B and I. That is certain. . .'

"'But!'

"'Hush! Be quiet! And since we are in a plain, and in that plain there is an immense mass of loose sand, the only place in which the train could have disappeared is in that mass of sand: *that is the eternal truth!*' . . .

"'I swear it didn't! I was at K waiting for the express; and I did not quit the line H I.'

"'By the immortal Masterpieces of the Italian Renaissance I command you not to let go of the right end of your Reason which I have put into your hand. We are discussing at this moment what *is*; we are not yet at the *how*. It is owing to the fact that you began with the *how* that you have not been able to reach what *is*. *The express is in I, since it cannot be anywhere else.* I am sure that the five men could not have seen it pass B, as they assert, unless it had passed. I am as certain that five men could not have been unable to see it at A if it had passed A; and since the line A B was examined and found not to contain the express, it must be that it turned off up the line H I. There we are, then, with the train on the line H I.'

"'But I was there too,' cried Theophrastus, 'and I swear to you *that it wasn't*!'

"'Dear! Dear! Do hold on to the right end of your Reason! You were at K; the express passed K; *it must pass K*; *it must go and plunge into I, since it cannot be anywhere else*. By a *necessary* chance, while the beginning of the train is engulfed in the mass of sand (I take it for granted that the line H I is too short for the engine-driver, having perceived the error of direction half-way up it, to have had the time to ward off the catastrophe), the couplings of the last carriage broke, and the carriage and the guard's-van began to descend the line which was on a slope since it went to this mass of sand. There, after having gone down the line to H and back up it to K, you saw the carriage and Signor Petito at the window. (Probably Signor Petito opened the window with the intention of jumping out, at the moment he grasped the imminent catastrophe, and as it happened the shock of it shut his head in the window.)'

"'That I understand; but what I don't understand. . .'

"'*Let us first consider what we do understand*: that is the right end of Reason. We will next consider what we do not understand. No one is found in the guard's-van. The shock undoubtedly hurled the guard into the sand. *All that is certain.* Now, after having stripped Signor Petito of his clothes, you sat down on the embankment and read his papers.

When you raised your head, the railway-carriage was no longer there. Well, since there was a slope and since there was a wind, which waggled the head of M. Petito at the window, the carriage, after having glided down to H, found itself once more on the line A B a little higher up than H on the side of B, where the staff of the station have by now certainly found it. *Do you understand now? Do you understand everything, except that you haven't seen the train pass K? Since everything is thus explained, it must be that that was how things happened.* Now I only seek how you were not able to see the train pass K. That which it is impossible to explain in the case of five persons at A or at B may very well be explained in the case of one at K.'

"'I am waiting,' said M. Longuet.

"I chuckled—and truly there was reason to chuckle—and went on, 'There are moments when you are deaf, M. Longuet?'

"'There certainly are,' said M. Longuet.

"'Suppose you were deaf during the moment you were waiting for the train at K, *then you would not have heard it*.'

"'No, but I should have seen it.'

"We have already arrived at the fact that you did not *hear it*. That is a considerable advance! God bless you, M. Longuet! God bless you!' (M. Longuet was sneezing.)

"M. Longuet thanked me for my pious wish, and since he continued to sneeze, I took out my watch from *his pocket* (he had already stolen it from me), and I said to him: 'Do you know, M. Longuet, how long a single one of your sneezes lasts, that is to say, how long you remain with your head bent while you sneeze? . . . Three seconds! . . . That is to say a second and two-fifths longer than is required to fail to see an express with four carriages pass in front of you, which is going sixty miles an hour. M. Longuet, the express has disappeared, or rather seemed to disappear, *because you were deaf and had a cold*!'

"M. Longuet threw up his arms wildly towards the ceiling of the Catacombs.

XXV

M. Mifroid Takes the Lead

When M. Longuet had recovered from the emotion with which my explanation of the disappearance of the express had filled him, he embraced me and handed me a revolver which he had found in the pocket of Signor Petito. He did not wish to keep it on him. He was desirous that I should be able, at need, to defend myself against the eccentricities of which he feared, on grounds based, alas! on a too real experience, the dangerous return. For the same reason he entrusted to me a large knife which had also come from the pocket of Signor Petito.

"We laughed; and then we set ourselves to consider our situation seriously. M. Longuet went on emptying his pockets; and there came out of them seven little electric lamps similar to those I had myself bought before falling into this hole. He congratulated himself, saying that his instinct had been right in urging him to take plenty of them, for, adding my six to his seven, we now had thirteen lamps, guaranteed to give forty-eight hours' light each, which gave us six hundred and twenty-four hours of consecutive light. He added that since we should not need light for the ten hours a day, afternoon—he was an advocate of the; restful siesta—and night, during which we should sleep, we had light for forty-four days eight hours.

"I said to him: 'You are altogether too old-fashioned, M. Longuet. Cartouche immured in the Catacombs would have done exactly the same with electric lamps as you are doing. But I, M. Longuet, I take your seven lamps and add three of mine to them; and this is what I do with them!'

"I threw them carelessly down against the foot of the wall.

"'There is no point in dragging about these *impedimenta*,' I said. 'Are you hungry, M. Longuet?'

"'Very, M. Mifroid.'

"'How long do you think you could be hungry?'

"Since he did not seem to understand, I explained that I meant to ask him how long he thought he could remain so hungry without eating.

"'I am pretty sure,' said he, 'that if I had to stay forty-eight hours as hungry as this. . .'

"'Let us suppose that you stayed as hungry as this for seven days,' I interrupted. 'Three lamps would be quite sufficient for us, for at the end of those three lamps we should have no need of light!'

"He had understood. But he smiled amiably, groped about, produced from the floor a good-sized parcel, and said:

"'But you see, M. Mifroid, I need not endure this hunger a moment longer than I need. I have here a ham which weighs ten pounds, or a hundred and sixty ounces. I am assured that if a man chews it in the manner invented by M. Fletcher of the United States, he can live for an unlimited period on four ounces of ham a day, and retain the full possession of his faculties and muscular power. We have therefore food for one man for forty days, food for two for twenty days. And then'—he paused, and a singular light came into his eyes—'I think, M. Mifroid, that then—at the end of that twenty days, *one of us will Fletcherise the other*!'

"'Nothing, M. Longuet, nothing would induce me to preserve my life by the degrading practice of cannibalism!' I said warmly.

"'It is a sentiment which does you much honour, M. Mifroid,' said M. Longuet. 'But there is no need, and indeed it would be impossible, that we should both become cannibals.'

"I was extremely disgusted, naturally, that M. Longuet should have been guilty of such an egregiously old-fashioned act as to be unable even to make an unexpected visit to the Catacombs, through a hole in the street, without bringing a ham with him; but I picked up the other ten electric lamps. I did not let my natural annoyance find vent in words; I only said to him, 'How on earth do you come to be walking about Paris with a ten-pound ham?'

"'I am going to write my memoirs,' said M. Longuet. 'And since quiet is necessary to the writing of one's memoirs, and I feared that you gentlemen of the Police would do your best to rob me of that peace, if I gave you the chance, I was going to shut myself in a little hiding-place I know of with this ham, these electric lamps, and some more necessary provisions which I had not yet bought, in order to write uninterrupted. The paper and pens I have already purchased; and they are in my hiding-place.'

"The excuse was valid, and there was nothing to be said. I set off down the passage.

"'Where are you going?' he said.

"'It does not matter where,' said I. 'But it is necessary to go anywhere rather than stay here, since here there is no hope. We will consider our course as we walk. Our only safety is in walking; and in walking for twenty days without taking any bearings we have every chance of arriving somewhere.'

"'But why without taking our bearings?' he asked.

"'Because,' I replied, 'I have remarked that in all the stories of the Catacombs it is always those bearings which have been the ruin of the unfortunate people who have got lost. They mixed up their bearings, were reduced to utter confusion, and fell into the exhaustion of despair. In our situation we must avoid every cause for despair. You are not in despair by any chance, M. Longuet?'

"'Not at all, M. Mifroid; I am only hungry. And I don't mind saying that if I were less hungry in your delightful society I should have no regrets whatever for the roofs of Gerando Street.'

"'We will eat presently, M. Longuet,' I said. 'An ounce of ham shall be our evening meal.'

"M. Longuet smiled hungrily; then he said, 'Perhaps it would blunt the edge of my appetite a little if you were to tell me something about these Catacombs.'

"'I think I ought to begin by giving you a general notion of the Catacombs,' I said. 'Then you would better understand why it is absolutely necessary to walk for a long time before getting out of them.'

"The road we followed was a long passage of from fifteen to twenty feet high. Its walls were very dry; and the electric light showed us a stone free from any parasitic vegetation, free even from any mouldiness. It was a sight which caused me some disquiet, for if we were to subsist for twenty days on a diet of salt ham, without any vegetable food, I feared that we might fall a prey to scurvy. My mind was at ease about the matter of drink; for I knew that in the Catacombs there were little streams of running water; and we had only to walk far enough to come across them.

"M. Longuet could not reconcile himself to the idea that we were walking *without caring where we were going*. I thought it wise to make him understand the necessity of not caring where we were going. I told him, as was the truth, that during the laying of the sewer the engineers, having descended into the Catacombs through the hole, had tried in vain to find their way about them and a way out. They had had to give it up, and to content themselves with building three pillars to prop up the roof, along the top of which their sewer ran, with materials let down through the hole by which we had so hastily descended, and which had been so definitely and unfortunately bricked up over our heads.

"Not to discourage him, I informed him that to my certain knowledge we could reckon on at least *three hundred and ten miles* of Catacombs, and that there was no reason that there should not be more. It was evident that if I did not at once make clear to him the difficulty of getting out, he would have yielded to despair at the end of a couple of days' journey.

"'BEAR IN MIND THEN,' I said, 'that they hollowed this soil from the third to the seventeenth century! Yes; for fourteen hundred years man has raised from under the soil the materials which were necessary for building on the top of it! So much so that from time to time, since there is too much on the top, and in places nothing at all beneath, the things on top have returned beneath whence they came.'

"Since we found ourselves under the ancient Quarter d'Enfer, I recalled to his memory that in 1777 a house in d'Enfer Street was in that way engulfed. It was precipitated a hundred and twelve feet below the pavement of its own courtyard. Some months later, in 1778, seven persons were killed in a similar landslip, in the district of Menilmontant. I quoted several examples of a later date, laying stress on the loss of life.

"He understood me and said, 'In fact, it's often more dangerous to walk about on the top than underneath.'

"I had gained his attention, and finding him so cheerful and interested, forgetting all about his hunger, I profited by it to quicken our steps; and I chanted the most spirited chorus I could remember. He took it up and we sang together:

'Step out! Step out, boys, with a will!
The road is hard and hot;
There's an inn beyond the hill
And good liquor in a pot!'

"That's the song that makes you step out!

"When we were tired of singing (one soon grows tired of singing in the Catacombs because the voice does not carry), M. Longuet asked me a hundred questions. He asked me how many feet of soil there were between us and the surface; and I told him that according to the last report it varied between eleven and two hundred and sixty feet.

"'Sometimes,' I said, 'the crust of earth is so thin that it is necessary to prolong the foundations of public buildings to the bottom of the Catacombs. Therefore in the course of our peregrinations there is a chance of our coming across the pillars of Saint-Sulpice, of Saint-Etienne-du-Mont, of the Panthéon, of the Val-de-Grâce, and of the Odéon. These buildings are, so to speak, raised on subterranean piles.'

"'Subterranean piles!' he cried joyfully. 'Is there really a chance that in the course of our peregrinations we shall come across subterranean piles?'

"Then he returned to his fixed idea:

"'And in the course of our peregrinations is there any chance of our coming across a way out? Are there many ways out of the Catacombs?' he said wistfully.

"'Plenty,' said I. 'In the first place, there are exits in the Quarter—"

"'So much the better!' he interrupted.

"'And others which are unknown, openings by which no one ever enters, but which none the less exist: in the cellars of the Panthéon, in those of Henri IV College, the Observatory, Saint-Sulpice Seminary, the Midi Hospital, some houses in d'Enfer, Vaugirard, Tombe-Issoire Streets; at Passy, Chaillot, Saint-Maur, Charenton, and Gentilly. . . More than sixty. . .'

"'That's good!'

"'It would have been better,' I replied, 'if Colbert had not on July 11, 1678—'

"'Wonderful!' interrupted M. Longuet. 'You have as fine a memory as M. Lecamus!'

"'It needn't astonish you, M. Longuet. I was formerly secretary of the Commissary of the district; and it pleased me to take an interest in the Catacombs, as it has since pleased me to practise the violin and sculpture. You have not got beyond the old-fashioned Commissary of Police, my dear M. Longuet.'

"He did not reply to that; he said, 'You were saying that Colbert on July 11, 1678—'

"'In order to put a stop to the cupidity of the builders, issued an order to close the openings into the Catacombs before Paris was quite undermined. That ordinance of Colbert's has, so to speak, walled us up.'

"At this moment we were passing a pillar. I examined the structure and said: 'Here is a pillar which was built by the architects of Louis XVI in 1778, in the course of the consolidation."

"'That poor Louis XVI!' said M. Longuet. 'He would have done much better to consolidate the monarchy.'

"'That would have been to consolidate a Catacomb,' said I felicitously, though I believe that the word Catacombs is only used in the plural.

"M. Longuet had taken the lamp from me, and without ceasing he turned its ray from right to left as though he were seeking something. I asked him the reason of this action which began to tire my eyes.

"'I'm looking for corpses,' he said.

"'Corpses?'

"'Skeletons. I have always been told that the walls of the Catacombs are lined with skeletons.'

"'Oh, that macabre tapestry, my friend (I already addressed him as 'my friend' because I was so pleased with his serenity in such serious circumstances), that macabre tapestry is barely three quarters of a mile long. That three quarters of a mile is very properly called the Ossuary, because skulls, ribs, shin-bones, thigh-bones, collar-bones, shoulder-bones and breast-bones form its sole decoration. But what a decoration! It's a decoration composed of three million and fifty thousand skeletons, which have been taken from the cemeteries of Saint-Médard, Cluny, Saint-Landry, the Carmelites, the Benedictines, and the Innocents. All the bones, well sorted, arranged, classified, and ticketed, form along the walls of the passages, roses, parallelograms, triangles, rectangles, spirals and many other figures of a marvellous exactitude. Let us desire, my friend, to reach this domain of death. It will mean life! For I do not know a spot in Paris more agreeably frequented. You only meet there engaged couples, couples in the middle of their honeymoon, lovers, and, in fact, all the happy people. But we are not there yet. What is three quarters of a mile of bones out of three hundred and ten miles of Catacombs?'

"'Not much,' he said with a deep sigh. 'How many miles do you think we have gone, M. Mifroid?'

"I begged him not to waste time in calculations which must be entirely futile; then, to cheer him up, I told him the story of the janitor and of the four soldiers. The first was very short: there was once a janitor of the Catacombs who lost his way in them; they found his body a week later. The second tells of four soldiers of the Val-de-Grâce who, by the help of a rope, descended a well two hundred feet deep. They were in the Catacombs. Since they did not reappear, they let down drummers who made all the noise they could with their drums. But since in the

Catacombs *sound does not carry*, no one answered the roll-call. They searched for them. At the end of forty-eight hours they found them dying in a cul-de-sac.

"'They had no moral force,' said Theophrastus.

"'They were idiots,' said I. 'When one is stupid enough to lose one's way in the Catacombs, one is unworthy of pity, I will go so far as to say, of interest.'

"Thereupon he asked me how I should myself escape losing my way in the Catacombs. Since we reached a place where another passage crossed the one we were in, I could answer without delay. I said:

"'Here are two passages, which are you going to take?'

"One of them ran directly away from our starting-point; the other almost certainly returned to it. Since it was our purpose to get away from our starting-point, M. Longuet pointed to the first.

"'I was sure of it!' I exclaimed. 'Are you quite ignorant of the experimental method? The experimental method in the depths of the Catacombs has demonstrated for centuries that every individual who believes that he is returning to his starting-point (at the entrance to the Catacombs) is moving away from it. Therefore the logical thing to do to get away from one's starting-point is necessarily to take the road which seems to bring you back to it!'

"We turned down the passage by which we appeared to be retracing our steps. In that way we were sure that we were not journeying in vain.

"My two stories had carried us over another mile; then M. Longuet said: 'I must really have my supper.'

"We had our supper, an ounce of ham each. There was some difficulty in judging how much an ounce was; but we did the best we could. He instructed me in the method of eating one's food discovered by M. Fletcher of the United States. We divided either ounce into four mouthfuls, not that they were by any means mouthfuls; and we chewed each patiently till we had extracted from it the last vestige of flavour. I could well believe him when he assured me that in this way we obtained from it the whole of the nourishment it contained. For my part, I should have been delighted to extract the last vestige of flavour from fifty more such mouthfuls.

"After this meagre, but doubtless exceedingly nourishing supper, we continued our journey. We went another four miles, when I confessed that I began to feel tired. I was somewhat surprised to find a manufacturer of rubber stamps, a sedentary pursuit, like M. Longuet to be endowed with such untiring vigour. On learning from my watch, which he still carried, because he said he found it a comfort to carry somebody else's watch, that it was eleven o'clock, I suggested that we should go to sleep.

"His fixed idea, that we should find an exit from the Catacombs, led him to display some reluctance. But I pointed out to him the extreme improbability of finding an exit in the first twenty miles of three hundred and ten; and we composed ourselves to rest.

XXVI

M. Longuet Fishes in the Catacombs

We awoke the next morning with the appetites of youth. In the middle of our exiguous breakfast it occurred to me that we were behaving in an extremely old-fashioned way. The heroes of Romance invariably divide their bar of chocolate into a number of pieces. We, with our ham, were showing ourselves as commonplace as they. I imparted these reflections to M. Longuet, and suggested that instead of making our hundred and fifty-eight ounces of ham last for twenty days, we should eat ten ounces each a day, and be content to let them last eight.

"M. Longuet objected firmly. He said:

"'In the first place the admirable discovery of M. Fletcher of the United States has proved that such a quantity of food is unnecessary for the sustenance of the human being.' (I learned later that this was a misstatement.) 'In the second place, it is our duty as French citizens to postpone the degrading practice of cannibalism to the last possible moment.'

"He spoke with a vigorous emphasis there was no gainsaying. I admired his strength of character, and was silent.

"Immediately after breakfast we resumed our journey.

"In about half an hour M. Longuet complained of thirst; and I explained to him that in our circumstances all complaints were utterly futile: a statement which, for all its undeniable logic, seemed to afford him very little comfort. But fortunately at the end of another hour our ears were greeted by the agreeable sound of rippling water; and presently the ray of our electric lamp gleamed on a little stream which ran from some subterranean spring across the passage. M. Longuet flung himself down and began to drink. I hesitated, for it appeared to me, as a logician, that since we could not carry water along with us, *to drink would only make us thirsty*. Then I reflected that we should find other springs, and presently followed his example.

"We went on our way; and presently M. Longuet inquired of me whether there was no nourishment of any kind in the Catacombs on which we might sustain life when we had exhausted the resources of ham and the survivor of cannibalism. Fortunately I had visited the laboratory of the Catacombs of M. Milne-Edwards; and I could entertain him with an account of the fauna and flora of these caverns, on which he would be able, at need, to keep himself alive. I am bound to say that, contrary to my usual habit, I took great pleasure in this conversation about edible things. I felt indeed that such a subject was extremely old-fashioned; doubtless my pleasure in it arose from the exiguity of my breakfast.

"'My dear friend,' I said, 'it is always possible not to die of hunger, even if you never get out of the Catacombs. The flora, the cryptogamic vegetation, the mushrooms, in a word, of the Catacombs, will not suffice, I fear, to keep you alive. But fortunately wherever you find water in these caverns, you find food. You can always become an ichthyophagus."

"'What on earth is that?' he said suspiciously.

"'An ichthyophagus is a fish-eater.'

"'Ah!' he exclaimed with an immense satisfaction, 'there are fish in the waters of the Catacombs! I am very fond of fish!' He paused; then he added in a musing tone, 'After all, it is better to be an ichthyophagus than a cannibal.'

"'They are not large fish; but certain streams contain incalculable quantities of them.'

"'Really? Incalculable quantities? . . . Incalculable? . . . How large are they?' he said with great animation.

"'Oh, they are of different sizes. Generally they are small. But they are not at all disagreeable to eat. I was told about them when I went down to visit the Fountain of the Samaritan, a very pretty, good-sized spring in the Ossuary.'

"'Is it far from here?' he said eagerly.

"'I cannot tell you at the moment. All I know is that this fountain was built in 1810 by M. Héricourt de Thury, Engineer of Subterranean Passages. As a matter of fact, this fountain is frequented by copepodes (Cyclops Fimbriatus). . .'

"'Ah! Copepodes! Are they fishes?'

"'Yes; and they present modifications of tissue and coloration peculiar to themselves. They have a beautiful red eye.'

"'What? One eye?'

"'Yes; that is why they are called cyclops. But you need not be astonished that this fish has only one eye, for the Asellus Aquaticus, which also lives in the running streams of the Catacombs, a little aquatic isopode, as its name indicates, often has no eyes at all.'

"'Impossible!' cried M. Longuet. 'How do they see?'

"'They have no need to see, since they live in darkness. Nature is perfect. She is perfect in giving eyes to those who need them; she is perfect in taking away eyes from those who do not need them.'

"M. Longuet appeared to reflect a little; then he said: 'Then, if we continued to live in the Catacombs, we should end by no longer having eyes?'

"'Evidently: we should begin by losing the use of our sight and then our sight itself. Our descendants would soon lose their eyes altogether.'

"'Our descendants!' he cried.

"We laughed at this little slip; and then he pressed me to continue my description of the fishes of the Catacombs.

"I discussed at length the modification of organs, their excessive development or their atrophy, according to the environment in which the species lives. I described the different kinds of fishes also at length.

"But at last he said: 'All this about their organs is very interesting. But how do you catch them?'

"'I can only tell you that the Catacombs which contain all these millions of bones cannot offer us a single maggot in the way of bait.'

"'No matter,' said Theophrastus. 'There are more ways of killing a dog than hanging him. An angler has more than one trick in his basket; and the Asellus Aquaticus had better look out.'

"That day and the days which followed it were very much alike. Whenever we came to a stream we stopped and drank. Always M. Longuet wanted to stop and fish. This was not wholly hunger; the sportsman's ardour burned in his soul. But I represented to him that, for anything we knew, we had the whole three hundred and ten miles of Catacombs to traverse before we came to the exit, and that it was our first duty to walk and walk. We might have fallen into them at the furthest end.

"By eleven o'clock, not only the sustaining but also the satisfying effect of the ounce of ham appeared to be exhausted; we were not only extremely hungry, but we were moving at a much slower pace. I represented to M. Longuet that it would be wise to have our déjeuner at once. But his dreadful middle-class instincts were too strong for us. He had the habit of a regular life so ingrained in him that he would not hear of déjeuner before noon. Also I marvelled at his power of endurance:

I had never suspected that the manufacture of rubber stamps could endow a man with those muscles of steel. None the less we talked very little between eleven and noon.

"That ounce of ham was one of the most delicious meals I have ever eaten. M. Longuet, who seemed in the course of our conversation to have caught some of my scientific spirit, timed the meal by my watch. It was a source of great satisfaction to him that he took from nine to eleven seconds longer over each mouthful than I did. After it we proceeded on our way with renewed vigour; and since I found that he was of the truly receptive type of mind, I found our conversation very enjoyable.

"The afternoon was exactly like the morning. We walked, conversing about a dozen different subjects. The next morning was exactly like the last afternoon; and the days which followed were exactly like one another. The second and third days were the least comfortable. On those days the satisfying effects of our ounces of ham appeared to exhaust themselves more quickly. But after the third day I began to realise the great value of the discovery of M. Fletcher of the United States. Our appetites had become quite normal; an ounce of ham blunted them till the next meal. We were losing weight indeed, especially M. Longuet, whose waistcoat hung somewhat limply down in front. But the muscles of our legs appeared to have grown stronger; and undoubtedly our intellects had grown quicker and more alert. When we had exhausted my subjects, I learned from M. Longuet the process of making rubber stamps, with a thoroughness which fits me to embark at any moment on that career. I found that he was even quicker to acquire the knowledge which goes to the making of an able Commissary of Police.

"It would indeed have been a very pleasant walking tour, thanks to that unlikeness of our natures which produces the most harmonious companionship, had it not been for the monotony of the scenery through which our way lay. The subterranean passages, illumined by our lamps, were sometimes vast, sometimes narrow, sometimes rounded like the naves of the cathedrals, sometimes square, angular, and mean, like the corridors of workhouses. But they presented no spectacle of great variety. When he had said, 'Look, stone! Look, clay! Look, sand!' we had said everything, because we had seen everything.

"It was on the afternoon of the fourteenth day that M. Longuet embarked on a subject of conversation extremely distasteful to me, the edible qualities of the human body. I tried gently to divert him from it; but it appeared to have become one of his fixed ideas; and he harped on it for two very tedious hours. That evening I halted for supper on the banks of a stream, nearly eighteen inches wide, which ran across the passage we were in; and after supper I suggested that, before retiring for the night, he should for once glut his sportsman's ardour.

"Though indeed he had no hooks, he fell to his angling with the liveliest eagerness. We turned the light of our lamp on to the waters of the stream, and presently out of the hole in the wall from which it issued, there came swimming a little fish. Then we found that hooks were unnecessary in the sport of the Catacombs. Owing to the fact that the little fish had no eyes, M. Longuet was able to lay his hand on the bed of the stream, which was, perhaps, at that point three inches deep, and when the little fish came swimming over it, to jerk up his hand and fling it on the bank. We examined his catch in the light of our lamp; but I was unable to say whether it was an Asellus Aquaticus or a Cyclops Fimbriatus.

"In the course of the next quarter of an hour we caught three more of these little fishes (they were nearly four inches long); then, at the sight of fresh fish, a wolfish gleam came into M. Longuet's eyes; and he suggested that we should repeat the supper we had only just finished. After his distasteful conversation of the afternoon, I made no objection. But with his ineradicable middle-class instinct he complained that we had no means of cooking our catch. I explained to him that our early ancestors, the cave-men, probably ate most of their food raw, and whatever else we were, we were, at the moment, undoubtedly cave-men. With this new intellectual alertness, acquired by following the method of M. Fletcher of the United States, he saw my point. We cleaned the fish with the knife of Signor Petito and ate them. They were delicious.

"But, as I should have foreseen, so much rich food coming suddenly after the rational diet on which we had subsisted during the last fortnight was too much for us, and for several hours we suffered the most acute pangs of indigestion. Moreover, with the greedy haste of gourmands, we had not timed ourselves over the meal, and had eaten the fish far too quickly. However, no experience is wasted on a rational man; and I realised that one Asellus Aquaticus, after ham, is enough for the logical Fletcherite.

"After the passing of our indigestion, we slept soundly; and the next morning we resumed our journey entirely free from any anxiety: it might take us six months, or it might take us a year, but sooner or later we should find the Ossuary and the exit from the Catacombs, sustained in our task by the Asellus Aquaticus. Indeed it was extremely improbable that it would take us more than a few days longer, for since I had never missed a chance of taking a passage which appeared to lead back to our starting-point, we must necessarily have drawn further and further from it.

"This expectation was realised sooner than I expected, for on the night of the seventeenth day, just as, at the close of a very interesting discussion on the neglect of the logical faculty by the great majority of men, we had turned our thoughts to supper and sleep, we were suddenly confronted by two skeletons.

"They were fastened against the wall on either side, and *an arm of either, like the arm of a finger-post, pointed down the passage ahead.*

XXVII

M. Mifroid Parts from Theophrastus

With a simultaneous cry of pleasure we quickened our steps, and presently we found ourselves between most interesting geometrical and ornamental figures composed entirely of bones.

"I took off my hat to those bones, with a sense of profound relief and gratitude. My stay in the Catacombs had been far from unpleasant, since I had passed the time in the company of such an agreeable and sympathetic companion; but I was glad that it had come to an end. I had had enough of it—possibly the monotony of the scenery had tired me of it. I had fallen into the way of instructing Theophrastus; and at once I taught him to distinguish between the tibia, the cubitus, and the femur. A knowledge of anatomy harms no one. But I was sorry to observe that he listened to me with an air of gloom. He did not seem to share my joy at reaching our journey's end.

"We had walked briskly for more than half an hour; and now and again I had paused to point out to Theophrastus some unusually artistic arrangement of the bones, when suddenly we came upon a lighted candle in the left eye of a skull. I concluded that we had at last reached the realm of the living. Then we came upon candles upon candles in the eyes of skulls, and then chandeliers full of twinkling candles. Then we heard voices: the babbling tinkling laughter of women. We were reaching the end of our journey.

"The first twentieth-century words we heard were:

"'Well, dear boy, this function isn't gay. I prefer the Bullier. . .'

"'Thank goodness, I'm only eighteen years old—a good long way from replacing these tibias!'

"We came into a big cavern to find ourselves in the middle of a fête. No one paid any attention to us; they took us for guests.

"All along those funereal walls were ranged rows of chairs. The light was bright, the candles and the chandeliers of skulls gleamed. At the end of the cavern was a platform covered with lines of music-stands. The musicians were just coming on to the platform. The audience was taking possession of the chairs; people were arguing and joking about the macabre decoration of the walls.

"All the cafés of the Abyss, all the artistico-mystico-macabre scenes in which life is laughed at and death jeered at, all those boxes of the Butte, in which skulls grin from the walls, and skeletons rattle on the floor, all the funereal carnival of Montmartre were surpassed.

"We had before us fifty musicians of the Opera, of Lamoureux, and of Colonne, who had come down into the Kingdom of Bones to serenade the Dead. And under the vaults of the Catacombs, among their avenues and crossways, where stretch the tragic walls covered with the bony wrecks of men, the funeral march of Chopin raised its lamentation before an audience of æsthetes, of artists, of Bulgarians, of Moldo-Wallachians, of frequenters of first-nights, of M. Mifroid, and M. Theophrastus Longuet, who sleeps peacefully on his chair as he always does at the theatre.

"'Perfect, that first violin! Perfect!' I said under my breath. (I am a connoisseur.)

"What gave me the greatest delight was the exquisite fashion in which the orchestra rendered the adagio of the third symphony of Beethoven. Finally we had 'The Dance Macabre' of Saint-Saëns. Then I tapped Theophrastus on the shoulder and said that it was time we went home. The concert after three weeks of the Catacombs had done me a world of good.

"We walked briskly, and ten minutes later we found ourselves on the surface of the earth. I breathed a deep sigh of satisfaction: with the exception of the ham, there had been nothing old-fashioned about our three weeks' journey through the Catacombs.

"'I told you that we should get out!' I said. 'My wife will indeed be pleased to see me!'

"'So much the better for you and for her,' said Theophrastus gloomily.

"'I should never have believed that the Catacombs were so pleasant,' said I.

"'Neither should I,' said Theophrastus gloomily.

"We walked on for a few minutes in silence. It was so pleasant to be walking under the open sky and the stars instead of under a roof in electric light, that I did not hurry to take a cab.

"Then Theophrastus said, 'What are you waiting for?'

"What am I waiting for? I'm not waiting for anything or anyone. I am being waited for. And I'm sure that Mme. Mifroid must be in a terrible state of anxiety.'

"'But why don't you arrest me? When I asked what were you waiting for, I meant what are you waiting for to arrest me?'

"'No, M. Longuet, no. I shan't arrest you. . . It was my mission to arrest Cartouche. But Cartouche no longer exists! There is only M. Longuet; and M. Longuet is my friend!'

"The eyes of Theophrastus filled with tears.

"'I have a strong feeling that I'm cured. . . if only I could be sure of it.'

"'What would you do if you were?' said I.

"'I should go back to my wife, my dear Marceline,' he said wistfully.

"'Well, you must go back to your wife, M. Longuet; you certainly must.'

"'You advise me to?'

"'Of course I do.'

"'No, M. Mifroid, no. She no longer expects me. Before falling through that hole in d'Enfer Street, I was careful to leave my clothes on the bank of a river. She believes me dead—drowned. She must be plunged in profound despair. My only satisfaction is that my dear friend, M. Lecamus, whom you know, has done everything possible for her in her affliction.'

"'That makes it all the more necessary for you to go back to her,' I said.

"'I will,' said Theophrastus; and his face brightened.

"We were shaking hands with one another, with the reluctance to separate of bosom friends; and indeed our sojourn in the Catacombs had made us bosom friends, when suddenly Theophrastus smote his brow and said:

"'*I must tell you a story of your youth!*'

"Now, if anyone, at such a time, with Mme. Mifroid in such a state of anxiety, had said to me, 'I must tell you a story of *my youth*,' I should have made some excuse and fled. But he said, '*I must tell you a story of your youth*.' It was extremely curious; I stopped and listened; and this was what he told me:

"'The incident took place in this spot, the Buci Cross-roads,' said Theophrastus.

"'Was I very young?' I asked, smiling.

"'Well, you must have been between fifty and fifty-five.'

"I gave a little jump. I am not quite forty. And you can understand my astonishment when M. Longuet spoke of an incident of my youth when I was between fifty and fifty-five. But he paid no heed to my movement, and went on:

"'At that time you had a greyish beard, cut into two long broad points which flowed gracefully down to your belt; and you were mounted—I can see it now—on a fine Spanish horse.'

"'Really? I was mounted on a Spanish horse?' (I have never been mounted on anything but a bicycle.)

"'A Spanish horse, which you gave to one of your archers to hold.'

"'Ah, I was in command of archers, was I?'

"'Yes, of twenty mounted archers, and a hundred archers on foot. All this troop had come from the Palais de Justice; and when it reached the Buci Cross-roads, you dismounted, because you were thirsty, and wished before the ceremony to get outside a pint at the tavern kept by the Smacker.'

"'And for what ceremony had I come from the Palais de Justice with my hundred and twenty archers?' said I, wishing to humour him, for I only wanted to get home.

"'It was the matter of summoning me by Public Proclamation for the murder of the workman Mondelot. Therefore on that day, March 28, 1721, the Clerks of Court, trumpeters, drummers, archers on horseback, and archers on foot, issued from the Palais de Justice in an imposing procession, and after having made the proclamation first in the Court de May, where everything passed quietly, and then again in Croix-Rouge Place, they came back here to the Buci Cross-roads. You had drunk your pint, M. Mifroid, and were mounting your Spanish horse, when this remarkable incident took place. The Clerk of Court read very solemnly: 'In the name of the King, through the Lords of Parliament, the said Louis-Dominique Cartouche. . .' when a voice, cried: 'Present! Here's Cartouche! Who wants Cartouche?'. . . On the instant the Clerks of Court, archers on foot, and archers on horseback, drummers and trumpeters, the whole procession broke up and fled in every direction. . . Yes; there did not remain a single person at the Buci Cross-roads, *not a single person except myself and the Spanish horse*, after I cried:

"'Here's Cartouche!'

"Phenomenon more curious than all curious phenomena in the depths of the Catacombs! . . . M. Longuet had no sooner said, 'Here's Cartouche!' than I started to fly from the Buci Cross-roads as fast as my legs could carry me, *as if the fear of Cartouche had dwelt in the calves of the police at the Buci Cross-roads for nearly two hundred years*!"

XXVIII

Theophrastus Goes into Eternal Exile

At this point I leave the report of the Commissary of Police, M. Mifroid. The conclusion of it indeed is filled with the most profound and philosophic reflections on the effect of companionship in misfortune on the human heart; but they are not relevant to the story of Theophrastus.

When the noise of the flying feet of M. Mifroid no longer came echoing down the empty street, the heart of that unfortunate man filled with the deepest melancholy. Here was that accursed Black Feather again! Behold him in the flickering light of a street lamp. He shakes his head. Ah! with what a lamentable air does he shake his miserable and dolorous head! Of what is he dreaming, unhappy wretch, that again and again he shakes his luckless head? Doubtless the idea he had had of going back to disturb the peace of his dear Marceline no longer appears to him reasonable. Plainly he rejects it, for his heavy, lagging feet do not carry him towards the heights of Gerando Street.

Some minutes later, he finds himself in Saint-Andrew-des-Arts Place, and plunges into the dark passage of Suger Street. He rings at a door. The door opens. In the passage a man in a blouse, with a paper cap on his head and a lantern in his hand, asks him what he wants.

"Good-evening, Ambrose. You are still awake, are you—as late as this?" said Theophrastus. "It's me. Oh, a lot of things have happened since I last saw you!"

It was true. A lot of things had happened to M. Longuet since he had last seen Ambrose, for he had not seen him since the day on which he had learned from him the date of the water-mark on the document found in the cellars of the Conciergerie.

"Come in, and make yourself at home," said Ambrose.

"I will tell you all about it to-morrow," said Theophrastus. "But to-night I want to sleep."

Ambrose took him up to bed, and he slept the dreamless sleep of a little child.

During the next few days Ambrose tried to induce Theophrastus to speak; but, oddly enough, he preserved a complete silence. He spent his time writing and writing. Once or twice he went out at night. Once Ambrose asked him where he was going.

"A Commissary of Police, M. Mifroid, is writing an account of a journey we took together," said Theophrastus. "And I am going to ask him for a copy of it."

I am inclined to believe that one of these nights he must also have returned to the flat in Gerando Street, by his favourite chimney, and taken away from it the report, which M. Lecamus had written for the Pneumatic Club, of the operation of M. Eliphas de Saint-Elme de Taillebourg de la Nox. Also on one of those nights he must have acquired the sandalwood box inlaid with steel; and since Ambrose believes that he had but little money, it is not improbable that when he acquired it he had his Black Feather.

One evening he came downstairs carrying a box, the sandalwood box, under his arm; and with an air of gloomy satisfaction, he said to Ambrose, "I have finished my literary labours; and I think I will go and see my wife."

"I did not like to speak to you about her," said Ambrose quickly. "Your gloom and your inexplicable behaviour made me afraid that you had some domestic difficulties."

"She is as fond of me as ever!" cried Theophrastus with some heat.

As he left the house, Ambrose said to him, "Be sure you remember me very kindly to Marceline."

Theophrastus said that he would; but to himself he said:

"Marceline will never see me; she must never see me. Not even the Catacombs have torn out my fatal Black Feather. I must not trouble her peace. She *shall* never see me. But I—I wish to see her once again, from afar, *to see if she is happy*."

He sobbed in the street.

It is nine o'clock at night, a dark winter's night. Theophrastus mounts the slope at the top of which rise the walls of Azure Waves Villa. With a trembling hand he draws back the bolt of the little door of the garden behind the house. He crosses the garden gently, noiselessly, one hand pressed against his heart, which is beating even more furiously than on the night of the purring of the little violet cat—his good heart, his great heart, still overflowing with love for the wife he wishes to see happy.

There is a light in the drawing-room; and the window is a few inches open, for the night is muggy. You advance slowly, noiselessly to a screening shrub, set down the sandalwood box, and peer through the leafless branches into the cosy drawing-room.

Ah! what have you seen in the drawing-room? . . . Why that deep groan? Why do you tear the white locks from your brow? . . . What have you seen? . . . After all, does it matter what you have seen, *since you are dead*? Did you not wish to see your wife happy? Well, you see her happy!

She and M. Lecamus are sitting on the sofa. They are holding one another's hand; they are gazing at one another with the eyes of lovers. He kisses her, with respect but with devotion. He is consoling her for the loss of you. You wished it. How can he better console her than by replacing you?

Theophrastus, the gentle, kind-hearted manufacturer of rubber stamps, perceives this. He drops on his knees on the cold, wet grass, weeping tears of bitter resignation. He is reconciling himself to the necessity of the cruel fact that they are sitting in his comfortable drawing-room, and he is kneeling on his cold, wet grass. He is almost reconciled to it; but not quite. What is that that is thrusting, thrusting forth? *The upward thrust of the Past—the Black Feather*!

The tears are drying in the eyes of Theophrastus. His eyes are gleaming through the dim winter night with an evil gleam. He springs to his feet; he grinds his teeth; he cries hoarsely:

"*By the throttle of Madame Phalaris!*"

The Past has him in its grip; he is racked by the pangs of the old-time jealousy, and the pangs of the new. In three seconds he is through the window and in the drawing-room. Wild screams of terror greet his entrance; but in ten seconds more M. Lecamus lies senseless in the big easy-chair, bound hand and foot with the bell-rope. When he recovers his senses, the hand of the clock has moved on ten minutes. Torn by fears and suspense, he listens with all his ears. He hears faint movements on the floor above. The minutes pass; twenty minutes pass. Then there is a sound of heavy footsteps on the stairs. Theophrastus enters, once more a changed Theophrastus: his eyes no longer gleam with an evil light; they are full of unshed tears. His face is working with intense emotion; and on his shoulder is a portmanteau.

What does that portmanteau contain?

Theophrastus, his face working with intense emotion, crosses the room to his old friend. He wrings his hand, wrings it for the last time; and in a broken voice, a voice full of tears, he says:

"Good-bye, Adolphe! Good-bye, dear friend, for ever! I am going to the *Seine near the Town Hall Bridge. I have to leave this portmanteau.* And then I go into eternal exile!"

He loosed his grip of his friend's hand and, his face still working with intense emotion, he went through the window, bearing the portmanteau with astonishing ease.

M. Lecamus has never seen him again; he has never seen Marceline again; he has never seen the portmanteau again. Does the unhappy Theophrastus, luckless exile from the Paris he loves, wander through the far East or the far West? Does he in the old eighteenth-century fashion police Bagdad, or does he build up a rubber stamp business in Chicago?

A Note About the Author

Gaston Leroux (1868–1927) was a French journalist and writer of detective fiction. Born in Paris, Leroux attended school in Normandy before returning to his home city to complete a degree in law. After squandering his inheritance, he began working as a court reporter and theater critic to avoid bankruptcy. As a journalist, Leroux earned a reputation as a leading international correspondent, particularly for his reporting on the 1905 Russian Revolution. In 1907, Leroux switched careers in order to become a professional fiction writer, focusing predominately on novels that could be turned into film scripts. With such novels as *The Mystery of the Yellow Room* (1908), Leroux established himself as a leading figure in detective fiction, eventually earning himself the title of Chevalier in the Legion of Honor, France's highest award for merit. *The Phantom of the Opera* (1910), his most famous work, has been adapted countless times for theater, television, and film, most notably by Andrew Lloyd Webber in his 1986 musical of the same name.

A Note from the Publisher

Spanning many genres, from non-fiction essays to literature classics to children's books and lyric poetry, Mint Edition books showcase the master works of our time in a modern new package. The text is freshly typeset, is clean and easy to read, and features a new note about the author in each volume. Many books also include exclusive new introductory material. Every book boasts a striking new cover, which makes it as appropriate for collecting as it is for gift giving. Mint Edition books are only printed when a reader orders them, so natural resources are not wasted. We're proud that our books are never manufactured in excess and exist only in the exact quantity they need to be read and enjoyed.

The Mighty Atom

The Mighty Atom

Marie Corelli

MINT EDITIONS

The Mighty Atom was first published in 1896.

This edition published by Mint Editions 2021.

ISBN 9781513283623 | E-ISBN 9781513288642

Published by Mint Editions®

minteditionbooks.com

Publishing Director: Jennifer Newens
Design & Production: Rachel Lopez Metzger
Project Manager: Micaela Clark
Typesetting: Westchester Publishing Services

to

THOSE SELF-STYLED "PROGRESSIVISTS,"

who by precept and example
assist the infamous
cause of

EDUCATION WITHOUT RELIGION

and who, by promoting the idea, borrowed from
french atheism, of denying to the
children in board-schools
and elsewhere,

THE KNOWLEDGE AND LOVE OF GOD

as the true foundation of noble
living,

ARE GUILTY

of a worse crime than murder.

Contents

I

A heavy storm had raged all day on the north coast of Devon. Summer had worn the garb of winter in a freakish fit of mockery and masquerade; and even among the sheltered orchards of the deeply-embowered valley of Combmartin, many a tough and gnarled branch of many a sturdy apple-tree laden with reddening fruit, had been beaten to the ground by the fury of the blast and the sweeping gusts of rain. Only now, towards late afternoon, were the sullen skies beginning to clear. The sea still lashed the rocks with angry thuds of passion, but the strength of the wind was gradually sinking into a mere breeze, and a warm saffron light in the west showed where the sun, obscured for so many hours, was about to hide his glowing face altogether for the night, behind the black vizor of our upward-moving earth. The hush of the gloaming began to permeate nature; flowers, draggled with rain, essayed to lift their delicate stems from the mould where they had been bowed prone and almost broken,—and a little brown bird fluttering joyously out of a bush where it had taken shelter from the tempest, alighted on a window-sill of one of the nearest human habitations it could perceive, and there piped a gentle roundelay for the cheering and encouragement of those within before so much as preening a feather. The window was open, and in the room beyond it a small boy sat at a school-desk reading, and every now and then making pencil notes on a large folio sheet of paper beside him. He was intent upon his work,—yet he turned quickly at the sound of the bird's song and listened, his deep thoughtful eyes darkening and softening with a liquid look as of unshed tears. It was only for a moment that he thus interrupted his studies,—anon, he again bent over the book before him with an air of methodical patience and resignation strange to see in one so young. He might have been a bank clerk, or an experienced accountant in a London merchant's office, from his serious old-fashioned manner, instead of a child barely eleven years of age; indeed, as a matter of fact, there was an almost appalling expression of premature wisdom on his pale wistful features;—the "thinking furrow" already marked his forehead,—and what should still have been the babyish upper curve of his sensitive little mouth, was almost though not quite obliterated by a severe line of constantly practised self-restraint. Stooping his fair curly head over the printed page more closely as the day darkened, he continued reading, pondering, and writing; and the bird, which had come to assure him as well as it could, that fine bright weather,—such weather as boys love,—might be expected tomorrow, seemed disappointed that its gay carol was not more appreciated. At any rate it ceased singing, and began to plume itself with fastidious grace and prettiness, peering round at the youthful student from time to time inquisitively, as much as to say,—"What wonder is this? The rain is over,—the air is fresh,—the flowers are fragrant,—there is light in the sky,—all the world of nature is glad, and rejoices,—yet here is a living creature shut up with a book which surely God never had the making of!—and his face is wan, and his eyes are sad, and he seems not to know the meaning of joy!"

The burning bars of saffron widened in the western heavens,—shafts of turquoise-blue, pale rose, and chrysoprase flashed down towards the sea like reflections from the glory of some unbarred gate of Paradise,—and the sun, flaming with August fires, suddenly burst forth in all his splendour, Full on Combmartin, with its grey old church, stone cottages, and thatched roofs overgrown with flowers, the cheerful radiance fell, bathing it from end to end in a shower of gold,—the waves running into the quiet harbour caught the lustrous glamour and shone with deep translucent glitterings of amber melting into green,—and through the shadows of the room where the solitary little student sat at work, a bright ray came dancing, and glistened on his bent head like the touch of some passing angel's benediction. Just then the door opened, and a young man entered, clad in white boating flannels.

"Still at it, Lionel!" he said, kindly. "Look here, drop it all for today! The storm is quite over;—come with me, and I'll take you for a pull on the water."

Lionel looked up, half surprised, half afraid.

"Does *he* say I may go, Mr. Montrose?"

"I haven't asked him," replied Montrose, curtly, "*I* say you may,—and not only that you may, but that you must! I'm your tutor,—at least for the present,—and you know you've got to obey me, or else—!"

Here he squared himself, and made playfully threatening gestures after the most approved methods of boxing.

The boy smiled, and rose from his chair.

"I don't think I get on very fast," he said, apologetically, with a doubtful glance at the volume over which he had been poring—"It's all my stupidity, I suppose, but sometimes it seems a muddle to me, and more often still it seems useless. How, for instance, can I feel any real interest in the amount of the tithes that were paid to certain bishops in England in the year 1054? I don't care what was paid, and I'm sure I never shall care. It has nothing to do with the way people live nowadays, has it?"

"No,—but it goes under the head of general information,"—answered Montrose, laughing,—"Anyhow, you can leave the tithes alone for the present,—forget them,—and forget all the bishops and kings too if you like! You look fagged out,—what do you say to a first-class Devonshire tea at Miss Payne's?"

"Jolly!" and a flash of something like merriment lit up Lionel's small pale face—"But we'll go on the water first, please! It will soon be sunset, and I love to watch a sunset from the sea."

Montrose was silent. Standing at the open door he waited, attentively observing meanwhile the quiet and precise movements of his young pupil who was now busy putting away his books and writing materials. He did this with an almost painful care: wiping his pen, re-sharpening his pencil to be ready for use when he came back to work again, folding a scattered sheet or two of paper neatly, dusting the desk, setting up the volume concerning "tithes" and what not, on a particular shelf, and looking about him in evident anxiety lest he should have forgotten some trifle. His tutor, though a man of neat taste and exemplary tidiness himself, would have preferred to see this mere child leaving everything in a disorderly heap, and rushing out into the fresh air with a wild whoop and bellow. But he gave his thoughts no speech, and studied the methodical goings to and fro of the patient little lad from under his half-drooped eyelids with an expression of mingled kindness and concern, till at last, the room being set in as prim an order as that of some fastidious old spinster, Lionel took down his red jersey-cap from its own particular peg in the wall, put it on, and smiled up confidingly at his stalwart companion.

"*Now*, Mr. Montrose!" he said.

Montrose started as from a reverie.

"Ah! That's it! Now's the word!"

Flinging on his own straw hat, and softly whistling a lively tune as he went, he led the way downstairs and out of the house, the little Lionel following in his footsteps closely and somewhat timidly. Their two figures could soon be discerned among the flowers and shrubs of the garden as they passed across it towards the carriage gate which opened directly on to the high road,—and a woman watching them from an upper window pushed her fair face through a tangle of fuchsias and called,—

"Playing truant, Mr. Montrose? That's right! Always do what you're told not to do! Good-bye, Lylie!"

Lionel looked up and waved his cap.

"Good-bye, mother!"

The beautiful face framed in red fuchsia flowers softened at the sound of the child's clear voice,—anon, it drew back into the shadow and disappeared.

The woods and hills around Combmartin were now all aglow with the warm luminance of the descending sun, and presently, out on the sea which was still rough and sparkling with a million diamond-like points of spray, a small boat was seen, tossing lightly over the crested billows. William Montrose, B.A., "oor Willie," as some of his affectionate Highland relatives called him, pulled at the oars with dash and spirit, and Lionel Valliscourt, only son and heir of John Valliscourt of Valliscourt in the county of Somerset, sat curled up, not in the stern, but almost at the end of the prow, his dreamy eyes watching with keen delight every wave that advanced to meet the little skiff and break against it in an opaline shower.

"I say, Mr. Montrose!" he shouted—"This is glorious!"

"Aye, aye!" responded Montrose, B.A., with a deep breath and an extra pull—"Life's a fine thing when you get it in big doses!"

Lionel did not hear this observation,—he was absorbed in catching a string of seaweed, slimy and unprofitable to most people, but very beautiful in his eyes. There were hundreds of delicate little shells knitted into it, as fragile and fine as pearls, and every such tiny casket held a life as frail. Ample material for meditation was there in this tangle of mysterious organisms marvellously perfect, and while he minutely studied the dainty net-work of ocean's weaving, across the young boy's mind there flitted the dark shadow of the inscrutable and unseen. He asked within himself, just as the oldest and wisest scholars have asked to their dying day, the "why" of things,—the cause for the prolific creation of so many apparently unnecessary objects, such as a separate universe of shells, for example,—what was the ultimate intention of it all? He thought earnestly, and, thinking, grew sorrowful, child though he was, with the hopeless sorrow of Ecclesiastes the Preacher, and his incessant cry of "*Vanitas vanita tem!*" Meantime, the heavens were ablaze with glory,—the two rims of the friendly planets, earth and the sun, seemed

Discover more of your favorite classics with Bookfinity™.

- Track your reading with custom book lists.
- Get great book recommendations for your personalized Reader Type.
- Add reviews for your favorite books.
- AND MUCH MORE!

Visit **bookfinity.com** and take the fun Reader Type quiz to get started.

Enjoy our classic and modern companion pairings!

Printed in the USA
CPSIA information can be obtained
at www.ICGtesting.com
JSHW082342140824
68134JS00020B/1828

9 781513 271965